TERRIFIC TALES

First published in Great Britain in 2010 by
Young Writers, Remus House, Coltsfoot Drive,
Peterborough, PE2 9JX
Tel (01733) 890066 Fax (01733) 313524
Website: www.youngwriters.co.uk

Foreword

Since Young Writers was established in 1990, our aim has been to promote and encourage written creativity amongst children and young adults. By giving aspiring young authors the chance to be published, Young Writers effectively nurtures the creative talents of the next generation, allowing their confidence and writing ability to grow.

With our latest fun competition, *The Adventure Starts Here …* , secondary school children nationwide were given the tricky challenge of writing a story with a beginning, middle and an end in just fifty words.

The diverse and imaginative range of entries made the selection process a difficult but enjoyable task with stories chosen on the basis of style, expression, flair and technical skill. A fascinating glimpse into the imaginations of the future, we hope you will agree that this entertaining collection is one that will amuse and inspire the whole family.

Contents

Invergordon Academy, Invergordon

Ivybridge Community College, Ivybridge

Lake Middle School, Isle of Wight

Sheldon School, Chippenham

The Ladies' College, Guernsey

William Ellis School, London

The Mini Sagas

Frightened

It was Saturday evening. I had finished sports late
and was walking through the forest. I heard a
noisy sound. I was frightened, thinking that it was
something huge and dangerous. I heard it again,
then out jumped a squirrel.
I burst into laughter when I saw this!

Rumbidzayi Makoni (13)

1

The Caterpillar

Later, I will be beautiful, but for now I will
continue my search for that green delight. Endless
days hunting for a goldmine of lush freshness.
Until satisfied I wrap myself in a silken cloak and
wait for that day of freedom to arrive.
Pop! A new world has begun!

Felicity Margereson (13)

The Picture

When Jo was little she heard noises from the
house next door. She went to the house, the
door opened by itself. She went into the rooms,
nobody had ever lived there.
A picture hung on the wall, she looked at it but
went through it, ending up in Wonderland!

Cecily Hart-Dunford (14)
Aegir Community School, Gainsborough

3

Predator Of The Night

In the middle of the night a grave keeper patrols
his graveyard. He spots an unusual crooked grave
lit by a blue flame. A shadowy figure appears from
behind and stabs its fangs into the grave keeper's
neck, draining him of blood.
A vampire has satisfied its lust for now!

Bryan Wilkinson (14)
Aegir Community School, Gainsborough

Sunbathing

The lizard would always sunbathe. It liked to sunbathe. When it sunbathed, nobody bothered it. The people didn't bother it. The predators didn't bother it. It was calm, quiet and peaceful. It soon fell asleep. When it woke up, the lizard jumped off the rock it was sunbathing on.

Sam Clark (15)

Aegir Community School, Gainsborough

5

Untitled

Once there was a boy. He never did anything because things were done for him. He never really wondered why he was so lucky. The truth was he wasn't lucky, he was dead. Because he was young when he died he had no sins and went to Heaven.
Lucky him!

Gemma Dooley (12)
Churchdown School, Churchdown

6

Mini Silly Sally

Silly Sally was mini. She went to see if she could see the top of the very tall tree. When she looked up, she fell back down to the very low, low ground and wondered if she would ever be able to see the top of the whole wide world!

Amy Jo Taylor (11)
Churchdown School, Churchdown

7

War Of Religion

Darkness alongside smoke and discomfort.
People were running in all different directions.
'Stop!' said a voice. 'We need peace in the world
and no wars. Religion doesn't matter, you can't
make everyone believe in your god, have the
pride and willpower to say no, walk away,' said
the voice.

Jess Waghorn (12)
Churchdown School, Churchdown

The Shop Of Croatia

She bought some shoes from the shop, very
expensive ones. She turned to shock, her
breathing had stopped. She had nothing to say but
a very large scream.
As a matter of fact it was one of her greatest
relatives from Croatia, what an exciting relief, she
couldn't believe it!

Macauley Medcroft (13)
Churchdown School, Churchdown

Alone

The moon shines, the stars twinkle, she sits alone.
The sun rises, the birds sing, she sits alone. The
trees sway, the bees hum, she still sits alone. The
air cools, the sky dims, she sits alone. She's seeing
black. She's feeling black. Her life's black.
Forever still, sitting alone.

Kim Phillips (12)
Churchdown School, Churchdown

The Deer

The lone deer drank peacefully from the watering
hole. As the other animals gathered and left, the
deer stayed. Then the deer caught sight of the
grass moving. The deer froze. The grass was
moving faster now. The deer's heart beating
faster. The grass opened. It was that armadillo
again!

Euan Jephcote (12)
Churchdown School, Churchdown

11

The Little Stream

Babble, babble, bubble, bubble, smooth shiny rocks
beneath, glittery ripples swirl around. Fish dart
and dive down deep. Frogs and insects love the
water clean and fresh with bubbles. The bubbles
look like drops of liquid diamonds. Soft silver and
grey, one of nature's benefits.
Nature, nature world of wonder.

Bethan Richards (12)
Churchdown School, Churchdown

Fairground

She will never go back there, since horses were
put there, galloping around, charging everywhere.
She will never go back there, since an ugly witch
has started to haunt it, and make scary noises.
She will never go back because of those things.
But she never ever did like fairgrounds.

Bethany Nutt (13)
Churchdown School, Churchdown

13

Them?

All is silent, all is right. All is black yet all is white.
Some are new, some are old. Some are brave,
some are bold. Why are they here? Why today? I
wish I knew what they had to say. I wish I knew
why they said, *'It has begun!'*

Cobi Ho (13)

Churchdown School, Churchdown

14

Boy Vs Computer

A young boy living his life to the full, doing his
English homework on the computer. An hour
passed staring into a screen of eternity. It came to
the time of printing - 'printer could not be found'.
'What do you mean, printer could not be found?
It's there you *idiot!*'

Ashley Loughran (13)
Churchdown School, Churchdown

15

The Moment

Heavy breathing, sweating, nervous, tears running, there's silence all around, he steps up, all eyes on him, about 100,000. *Boom,* the object flies through the air to its difficult target, people breathless then ... '*Yesss,* get in there, son! 2-1 to the champion! 2-1 to the champion!'

James Benfield (14)
Churchdown School, Churchdown

Lost Forever

I'm less than air, in fact I'm nothing, I'm lost.
Nobody can see me and nobody can hear me, so
what am I? I am so cold I can feel the air rushing
against me. I'm scared, please help me.
Am I dead? Yes or no? I'm lost forever!

Chloe Young (13)
Churchdown School, Churchdown

Mummy!

'Am out!' she roared.
'OK Mummy,' replied a little voice.
'Am back!' she roared again.
'Yay, Mummy's back,' said a little voice.
'Am hungry!' she roared.
'Yes Mummy,' said a little voice.
'Am eating now,' she roared again.
The little voice didn't reply, it was silent. She roared again.

Manuela Ifedolapo Alli (14)
Churchdown School, Churchdown

Psycho

I had a bow and arrow and a knife. Someone
was behind me. I turned round and killed them
... Blood dripped off my knife. It was my mum so
I went on a killing spree. I killed everyone then
myself.
I woke up! It was a dream.

Anthony Dunlop (13)
Churchdown School, Churchdown

19

Don't Try This At Home

Billy watched as the two men tried to kill each
other. But all he did was watch and smile. The
two men just kept on fighting and Billy just kept
on watching and smiling. Billy started to cheer
them on very loudly.
'Turn off the TV!' Billy's mum loudly shouted.

James Summers (13)
Churchdown School, Churchdown

Snatched

1950, she went to bed one night and never woke
up. Snatched at twelve and never came back!
2,000, fifty years later, no sign of her, just many
strange happenings around that area.
Her mother always sees her, her father does too.
In Heaven they are, all happily together forever.

Lauren McLean (12)
Churchdown School, Churchdown

Untitled

At midnight, in the garden, red eyes stared at me
in despair, with the moonlight which lit the eyes
up like a demon.
Then suddenly I heard something; 'Shane could
you let the dog in please?'

Shane Hinder (13)
Churchdown School, Churchdown

22

Horror Down The Street

It was late at night and I had decided to get a pasty. I turned around in a deserted street to hear an ear-piercing scream coming from the house ahead ... I went in to find two boys watching a horror movie.

Jack Tandy (12)
Churchdown School, Churchdown

Bloodthirsty Dog

The bloodthirsty dog spotted a petrified cat. The dog ran after the cat. *Pounce!* The cat ran into a nearby house. The cat was pouring with blood. His body parts were everywhere. The cat was no more!
Alone, just sat there, helpless.

Lucy Southgate (12)
Churchdown School, Churchdown

The Friendly Loch Ness

Andrew was bored, he thought it was just stupid
waiting for nothing. As he got up, the ground
shook then it stopped. Andrew stood petrified,
dared to turn around. A green scaly monster was
staring at him. Andrew's heart was pounding ...
'Hello, would you like a ride?'
Andrew smiled, 'OK!'

Sam Powell (13)
Churchdown School, Churchdown

Terror

I was in terror as the bright red eyes stared at me. I quickly cowered into a corner. Steam was filling the room. I started to turn pale as the dreadful beast stomped towards me ...
I wish that I hadn't told her that she looked fat in that dress!

Isaac Wright (13)
Churchdown School, Churchdown

Road To Victory

They marched for so long. Beaten, bruised but they never stopped until they came to the road of victory. 'I have a dream!' Martin Luther King said. *Bang!* But we never stopped marching.

Chilombe Daka (14)

Churchdown School, Churchdown

Goldilocks And The Three Bears

Mum Bear made porridge, hot, warm, cold.
Goldie smelt them and gobbled them up. Later
she found three beds; too lumpy, too hard, just
right. She fell asleep.
The bears came back, found her in the bed and
chased her all the way home.

Tamzyn Davis (13)
Churchdown School, Churchdown

Cutting Squares

I was in my house, baby asleep upstairs. I heard
a voice so I went upstairs. My baby was fine.
I turned around, I heard the voice, 'Cutting
squares, cutting squares. I like cutting squares.'
I turned around, my baby was cut into squares!
'Cutting squares, I like cutting squares.'

Alexandros Legal (14)
Churchdown School, Churchdown

29

The Minotaur

'Slay the evil Minotaur,' said King to Soldier.
So Soldier headed to the maze where the evil
creature lurked.
'Please don't slay me, I'm just like you.'
'Don't be ridiculous.'
The Minotaur, it fought back and killed Soldier.
But then he used Soldier's knife to remove the
glued-on mask.

Wileey Adla (14)
Churchdown School, Churchdown

The Crash!

I sit holding my steering wheel. Big crowds
watching. My heart pounding. My first F1 race.
The green light goes on, F1 cars racing round the
track! 5th! 4th! 3rd! 2nd! 1st! I am in the lead.
Crunch!
My car is flipping through the air ...

Shaun Wall (14)
Churchdown School, Churchdown

The Night Of Bombing

The bombs came fast. I wasn't ready, nobody was. We ran into a bomb shelter and waited. Waiting for everything to stop. It was crowded, too crowded. People started to leave, they couldn't cope. I could cope. I had to. 'I will make it, I will,' I said to myself.

Nicole Russell (13)
Churchdown School, Churchdown

Could I Ever Get Out?

I walked down row after row. It was like a maze
to me. A maze that never ended. It would take
forever to find the way out. I would have to pay
for coming here. I hate the supermarket.

Luke Gammon (13)
Churchdown School, Churchdown

21st Century Cinderella

'Ma lady, come back!' Cinderella disappeared into the dark. The prince found the glass shoe and thought, *this should sell for a bit on ebay.* Then she came back, slapped him and said, 'Only £6 at Primark!'

Coby Andrews (12)
Churchdown School, Churchdown

Thirsty Desert

The man sped through the desert, getting slower
and slower until he fell to his knees. He gasped
for air and he begged for something cooling, even
a simple breeze. His throat was dry.
Suddenly he spotted a lake, there was Heaven!

William Turner (12)
Churchdown School, Churchdown

35

Brithday Shoot-Out!

It was intense. I had my gun close to me - trigger ready. I heard heavy breathing. This was it. 'Die!' I shot randomly in front, hoping for the best. There was a loud moan. I hit the target! +50 points. Yes! Laser-Tag was great. Best birthday I've had.

Samuel Thompson (13)
Churchdown School, Churchdown

Teeth

A shark saw a small child on his own. The shark swam silently towards the boy. The shark was close to the boy, savouring the meal to come. Then *crash!* The shark smashed into the glass of his container.

Andrew Henwood (14)
Churchdown School, Churchdown

Nazi-Zombies

On the playing field of battle, horror and death, there's one thing that haunts the soldiers of the opposing side of war. Nazi-zombies. They raise terror in every nook and cranny of the battlefield. They are Hitler's creepy invention, an invincible, never-ending army of zombies ... Will we survive?

Aaron Gobey (13)
Churchdown School, Churchdown

The Run

He was sprinting as fast as he could. He was
sweating, scared of what was behind him. He
was terrified of getting caught. He was starting to
shake, he had to stop! He carried on ...
and by a miracle crossed the finish line
in first place.

Jack Carr (14)

Churchdown School, Churchdown

The Chase

It was freezing cold. All you could see was the steam coming off the sprinting rabbit. It was getting chased constantly by the bloodthirsty fox. The fox was persistent and was getting closer. Then there were two sharp gunshots. The rabbit and fox lay dead as stones.

Ben Mumford (14)
Churchdown School, Churchdown

Too Small

'Oh no! It's way too tight, it hurts,' screamed
Emma! *What should I do?* she thought to herself.
Then she realised her dress was a size too small
and that she was in a dressing room!

Danielle Evans (14)
Churchdown School, Churchdown

The Cake Shop

Billy went to buy some cakes and saw Tod at his
gate so they both went to buy some cakes. When
they got there the shop got robbed.
So poor Billy and Tod had no cakes.

Matthew Cushnan (13)

Churchdown School, Churchdown

The Seeker

Horrifying, too hot for human life form. The stench of rotting fish all around. He couldn't take it any longer. Sickness inside him was growing. Then, from the darkness, a figure stood in front of him. 'Found you!' she laughed. 'You'll have to do better than your wardrobe!'

Becky Turner (12)

Churchdown School, Churchdown

43

Untitled

He ran away from the market to the farm, chased by soldiers. He dropped. They dragged him back to the castle to his death. I looked at him, his eyes bloodshot. A sway of the axe. A drop. A roll. His eyes could've burst. We'll never know will we?

Emma Cahill (13)
Churchdown School, Churchdown

Untitled

I was sitting on my own at home. I was very cold.
There was a tiptoe noise coming from upstairs.
I didn't know what to do. I went upstairs, there
was a cat. I went into the bedroom. *'Argh!'* A man
hanging in cold blood. What should I do?

Matt Mills (12)

Churchdown School, Churchdown

45

Nemo

A couple of clownfish had eggs; they got eaten except the dad and an egg. The egg grew up and went to school, got caught by fishermen and put in a fish tank. Girl bought it, tried to kill it, tried to act dead, came alive again and went home again.

Kate Yarnton (14)

Churchdown School, Churchdown

Mini Marvels Terrific Tales

The Love

She was walking along the road, minding her own business when she was grabbed from behind, she could feel cold breath on her neck. He spun her around. Stared at her in the eye and said ...
'So how was your day?'
'Fine,' then kissed her gorgeous boyfriend passionately.

Rebecca White (14)
Churchdown School, Churchdown

47

The Game

Saturday, the big game. Baseball, the best. Steve and Ron had won tickets in a competition to write a story. They were looking forward to it. The stadium was huge. So was the pitch. Lots of people were there. The ticket man said, 'Sorry lads, the game was last week!'

Kayleigh O'Connor (14)
Churchdown School, Churchdown

Bounce

I went so high, I was so scared, all my friends had abandoned me. I was alone, so high, so high. I felt like I was going to die. I started to fall. I landed with a squish on the trampoline.
'Who's next? You pick.'
My mum said, 'Right then.'

James Blackshaw-Dobbins (11)
Churchdown School, Churchdown

49

A New Life

2021, the time of evolution. Humans evolved by injection, we had no means of evolving, we had travelled universes not as our original form. Darwin, when living, thought we were apes. We don't now look like apes, he'd be devastated! 2931, the second Roman Empire. Life started again, not time.

Alexander Hitchman (12)
Churchdown School, Churchdown

Honey, I'm Home

Mother and son were sitting on the settee on a Saturday night. Dad still at work till 6 o'clock. The door opened with a breeze. Mother and son were *very* scared. All sorts of things were running through their minds, *ghost, spirit, zombie? What could it be?*
'Honey, I'm home!'

Charlie Hobbs (12)
Churchdown School, Churchdown

51

Tut, Tut, Tut

Why did this have to happen to me? I did all my homework, why did it happen? I got a detention, my mum is going to flip. I hate my school and the stupid teachers. But I can see why I got the detention. I only wrote one sentence!

Jake Wolstencroft (12)

Churchdown School, Churchdown

Tall Annabel And The Small Daffodil

Annabel Tall was born tall. She remained tall.
Handles were too low down, windows were a
ledge too low, libraries were an open book. She
longed to see another tall person, eye to eye.
When she died they buried her under a daffodil.
A few years later, she couldn't see.

Lauren Knight (12)
Churchdown School, Churchdown

53

Little Girl Don't Cry

1981. Dear James,
This foster home is killing me. The food is
horrible and there is no TV, and the only time
we are allowed out is on Wednesday but that is
Project night to do my homework! Please James, I
am begging you to save me from here, please!'

Jasmine Locke (11)
Churchdown School, Churchdown

54

Game Over

Bang! The sound boomed around the room.
Blood trickled out of his lifeless body as he fell to
the cold hard floor. Just one shot could snatch life.
Not again, I thought to myself as the words
Game Over appeared on my TV screen.
'Bet I'll do it,' boasted Ben.

Jake Collins (13)
Invergordon Academy, Invergordon

The Mission

I crept through the shanty houses, *bang!* Concrete was torn in two like a foil wrapper. All around me gunfire raged. Metal penetrated my leg. My partner helped me up. The empty barber's shop provided good cover. My gun was ready to fire ... Suddenly, 'Get off that PlayStation, Joe!'

Ben Reeve

Invergordon Academy, Invergordon

I Need Food!

I need food, I'm starving. A rabbit, mice, anything.
My tummy thunders. You can see my ribs. I need
food! I've got a target. Six tasty chickens, snoring
quietly, fast asleep. Three more steps. *Crash!*
Gulp! Down they go. Time to hide, before an
angry farmer reaches for his *gun!*

Kerry Cartwright (13)
Invergordon Academy, Invergordon

57

Seven Long Awaited Words

Friday night. Half of Britain glued to channel 1. The theme tune resounded to a nation full of anticipation. The first live episode. A 25th birthday. A storyline gripping the nation. An awful addiction. The seven long awaited words came from Stacey Slater, 'It was me, I killed Archie Mitchell!'

Nina Wilson (13)

Invergordon Academy, Invergordon

Big Sir And Number 29

'*Bawk*, I'm stuck!' shouted Lintus.
'We'll save you!' screamed Big Sir and No 29
together. They darted up onto the roof, untied
Lintus and brought him down to safety.
Atticus ran outside wondering what had
happened. 'Nothing at all,' they squawked in
unison as they ran back into their pen.

Avene Nicolson (12)

Invergordon Academy, Invergordon

Yes We Can

I watched the results in my overly lavish sweat. A big, excited crowd cheered. I won. I did it, I was absolutely speechless, just on cloud nine. I am the one, I'm in charge. I made history.
The only bad thought was would the pressure be too much for me?

Luke Cormack (13)
Invergordon Academy, Invergordon

Mini Marvels Terrific Tales

Winner

Nervously, Sam placed the £50 bet, his life savings. The horses shot out of the gate. After three laps his chosen mount was only midfield. Distraught, Sam glanced down. Then the crackling tannoy announced Clover, his horse, the winner at 100-1!

His mother would get the wheelchair after all.

Freya Dane (12)

Invergordon Academy, Invergordon

Blazing Manchester

I looked out the window at Manchester falling to pieces. 'Billy, come on,' called Mom. I had to leave for the shelter. We took our dog, Max. We'd never leave him behind. So we ran and ran and ran.

Boom! I found myself in a pile of rubble.
So ... quiet ...

Owen MacFadden (13)
Invergordon Academy, Invergordon

How Tedious Is He?

He swims around in a circle or he's sleeping in his castle when an occasional bubble floats to the surface. He stares at the same surroundings every day for hours on end. He eats the same brown flakes every day. He beats me at staring contests always. *Grr* ... Stupid goldfish!

Matthew Ilett (12)

Invergordon Academy, Invergordon

63

The Hunt

Bang! Bang! That rabbit was just too fast. He ran and ran, dodging the trees until he was puffed out ... *Bang! Bang!* It was no good. The rabbit had disappeared. He would just have to come back the next day. Hungry and disappointed he slowly dragged himself sadly back home.

Saffron Ross (12)

Invergordon Academy, Invergordon

He's Flying

5, 4, 3, 2, 1, Robbie trotted as fast as his wee legs could take him. His friends snorted at him. He was never going to fly. Robbie got to his ramp. He opened his legs wide and jumped. His friends gazed. He was flying! He looked up, 'Hey Seagull!'

Gemma MacLean (13)

Invergordon Academy, Invergordon

Yum!

Merge dolphin, butter and sugar. Combine doves'
eggs and flour. Infuse me with papaya, passion
fruit and pineapple. Add drops of vanilla essence,
a sumptuous mixture, stir honey and blend.
Serve the luxurious fusion into pink cases. Pop me
in the oven. Watch me rise. *Yum!*
I am a tropical cupcake.

Lucie Martin (12)
Invergordon Academy, Invergordon

My Pet

A wagging tail and a wet nose, bouncing, running,
fetching and barking. On a walk, having fun,
mucky paws and mucky face. Curling up to have
a nap before bounding around the garden once
more. Biscuits, treats and toys galore.
It is just a dog's life for my pet, Daisy.

Stuart Ham (12)

Invergordon Academy, Invergordon

67

My Shining Beauty

'Deal!' says the man in a dark posh suit, shaking
my hand professionally. I stare at my shining
beauty and whistle, I'm soaring away listening to
her gentle purring and the steady rhythm of her
heart. We come to a halt.
'Wow, nice car, man!' a boy in rags exclaims.

Ellie Carr (12)
Invergordon Academy, Invergordon

Light As A Feather

Blast-off, 5, 4, 3, 2, 1 ... The rocket shot up into space at a thousand mph. They were scared because they were going at such a speed up into nowhere. *Zzz!* An electronic door opened and a wire came out. They were ready to explore the solar system!

Andrew Francis (12)

Invergordon Academy, Invergordon

69

Spots

Slinking closer, closer, eyes fixed, so hungry,
more silent than a mouse and twice as agile,
nearly there! The earth beneath its paws. A flash
of spots and the race has begun, twist and turn,
faster, faster.
A fatal trip! Now is its chance. The cheetah has
caught the gazelle.

Emily Marshall (13)
Invergordon Academy, Invergordon

The First Teddy

Not a shot that day. He felt embarrassed. He did not dislike this creature. He didn't want to harm it in any way. So why? He looked at the terrified creature tugging ineffectively at the ropes. Feeling his fists clench he took a knife. The rope was cut. Freedom again!

Eilidh Munro (12)
Invergordon Academy, Invergordon

Mission; Possible

'Hawk, move in round the back.'
'Moving in.'
'On my mark, 3, 2, 1, go!'
Time to distract the protector. *Crash! 'Oww!* I've
fallen off my bike! *Help!'*
Mum thunders round the corner. Behind her
Hawk sneaks into the den. Seconds later he's out
with the prize: cookies. Chocolate chip!

Iona Mathieson (12)
Invergordon Academy, Invergordon

Toasted

They love keeping us warm and toasty. No need
for a jacket or a crazy hat. They make us feel snug
as if wrapped tight in a cosy blanket. They keep
our toes heated in the morning when we wake
up.
How did we ever live without them?
Radiators - genius!

Hannah Drummond (13)
Invergordon Academy, Invergordon

73

The Dog

The dog ate the dictionary, my one and only book. He grabbed it with his sharp teeth and shook and shook and shook. I tried to take him for a walk, but no, he definitely would not have that. Now I'm beginning to wonder why I didn't get a cat.

Joe Pennington (13)

Invergordon Academy, Invergordon

On The Run

The blood, the pain, the fear. The pup stopped,
ears perked. Was that a voice she just heard? One
swift movement and the wolf was behind her, she
whimpered, running for dear life.
The wolf was too fast, with a few graceful strides
he was upon her and then ... silence.

Eleanor Davies
Ivybridge Community College, Ivybridge

Luggage?

'Where's my luggage? It isn't here.' I got handed my tea by the suspicious hostess. It was like she knew something I didn't. I asked, 'Where's my luggage?' She paused and just continued, she knew something about my luggage.
I got woken, and the hostess asked, 'Want a drink, Sir?'

Mason Hughes (13)
Ivybridge Community College, Ivybridge

It's Just Another Day

I wake up. I hear the crying voices of the lonely
civilians. Wind sweeps in with the horrendous,
torrential rain. I fire my rifle with great contempt.
I watch my fellas go on with great courage.
People dying, one by one. But I know deep down,
it's just another day.

William Wentworth (13)

Ivybridge Community College, Ivybridge

The Sparrow

There once was a bird, sat in a tree, too scared
to fly, too scared to flee. For there was a hawk,
its beak shining bright, floating there ready, to
pluck any birds from flight. For there in the tree,
unfurling its wings, using its last moment, started
to sing ...

Jonny White (12)
Ivybridge Community College, Ivybridge

The Charge

Guns were blazing, rain falling. The whistle
blew, men falling, blood raining down on me.
Mines blowing. I hid in a crater. Men charging,
screaming, shouting for their lives. My best friend
was hit,
I ran towards him to defend his life, it was
too late ... The game was over.

Ryan Baugh (12)
Ivybridge Community College, Ivybridge

79

A Teenager Drinking Alcohol

Out with mates. Someone will buy us a drink.
Can't wait to get drunk, it won't be that bad.
Called Jake, met him at the park at 11pm. I got
this guy to buy me some drink. We were drunk
by 11.30pm. One bad moment. I got sick over
me.

Callum Murphy (13)
Ivybridge Community College, Ivybridge

The Corridor

Pathelonius cautiously crept down the winding
passageway, his sword gripped firmly in his hand,
ready to strike; his other hand ahead of him
feeling the walls as it was pitch-black.
He grasped a doorknob, he opened the door,
it appeared: blood-red, ferocious beast,
Pathelonius lunged forward ...

Vincent Smith (13)

Ivybridge Community College, Ivybridge

Nowhere To Hide!

She was running, swerving and dodging trees, running straight for safety. As she entered, she turned, locking the door fast, ran to lock the backdoor, then ran upstairs to her room and turned the lights off. A rustle of the curtains and a voice said, 'Tag, you are it.'

Tyler Colton (13)
Ivybridge Community College, Ivybridge

Luggage Affair

'Where is it?'
'Where's what?'
'There's three suspects to this case and you're
the main one!'
'Okay, okay I'll do it, I'll tell you everything.'
'Good, now spill … '
'Everything was fine, I was just doing my job.'
'Stop crying girl, where is it?'
'Stop shouting, I'll tell you … Terminal Five!'

Olivia Smith (13)
Ivybridge Community College, Ivybridge

83

Maci-D's, But Shorter!

Alan's life was rubbish: from his skyscraper flat to his job at McDonald's, everything was miserable. Then he was sacked!
He got a job at a restaurant, GastroDish, but he got a surprise: the owner was like him. Alan left, and guess what? Now he has his own restaurant. Nice!

George Jones (12)
Ivybridge Community College, Ivybridge

The Froggy

There was a wicked froggy, he looked really cool,
he spent all his day sitting on a toadstool. Then
one day his toadstool collapsed. Would he find
another? Maybe, perhaps.
Then one day he found a toadstool and then once
again he looked really cool, the froggy had it all.

Andrew Low (12)

Ivybridge Community College, Ivybridge

85

Hunger Strike

Walking along, skipping a little. No one about.
Quarter to twelve. Shouldn't be here now. People
will wonder, *who is that kid?* Been here too long.
Don't know what to do. Waiting. What for? I
could be here 'til morning. And the clock strikes
twelve. Yeah! At last, it's lunchtime!

Georgia Pink (12)
Ivybridge Community College, Ivybridge

Clutches Of Death

The path twisted and turned as the gazelle
avoided the clutches of death. The cheetah licked
its lips as it maintained its perfect balance.
Then, out of nowhere, the lion pounced and rode
the cheetah's back. The cheetah was dead!
The lion shrank back into the wilderness with
its prey ...

Max Tipping (12)

Ivybridge Community College, Ivybridge

The Race For Life

I'm running. My legs are aching. I turn to watch the black figure following me, closing. I try to avoid the many trees. The only light is coming from the moon. I can see my house but I can also hear the heavy footprints. Yes, I'm there, I win.

Oliver Hudson (13)

Ivybridge Community College, Ivybridge

There Was A Ghost

He lived in a mine. He had no friends. He had no wine. When one day the mine flooded. He swam and swam until ... he landed in a vineyard, he saw a shop which sold wine. When he went in, everyone screamed. He had no friends but lots of wine.

Sacha Walton (11)
Ivybridge Community College, Ivybridge

Clueless

I crept slowly towards the haunted cottage. I opened the broken door, the open room infested by cobwebs. In the corner of my eye I could see a sparkling charm glimmering on the wall. It hypnotised me. Suddenly cold hands grabbed my arms and then it bit me! I screamed.

Tilly Loveland (11)
Ivybridge Community College, Ivybridge

The Monster's Revenge

'Walk slowly towards me and whatever you do,
don't look back.'
Jinny started to walk forwards then glared at me.
'Is this some kind of trick?' she asked spitefully.
'No!' I replied, but she didn't believe me and
turned around. Suddenly the hideous monster
whipped her up.
'Heeeelp!' she screamed.

Carli-Ann Wilcott (12)

Ivybridge Community College, Ivybridge

The Leafy Caterpillar

One day there was a caterpillar called Jimbobin and he had a leaf which he took with him everywhere, but one day there was something wrong. There was a hole in the leaf and Jimbobin couldn't survive with a holey leaf, and he couldn't replace it, so he passed away.

Emily Soper (12)
Ivybridge Community College, Ivybridge

Untitled

Rubber Ducky was floating along when, all of a sudden, it all went wrong. He flapped his wings and flew away. Then he came back another day. Yellow with an orange beak. Squeaks every time he hits something big, like rocks almost hard, cuts and bruises - he carries on going.

Charlotte Myers (12)
Ivybridge Community College, Ivybridge

93

Humpty-Dumpty's Haunted House

The day I turned twelve was the day I'm sure I died, but before I'd never been hurt by anything more than a fly! Until my twelfth birthday when I rescued my best friends. I gave my life to ensure that Humpty-Dumpty's haunted house was never visited again!

Sophie Etherton (12)
Ivybridge Community College, Ivybridge

The Unknown Forest

Tom was pushed by Matt into the forest! Every person knew not to go in the forest, however Tom was there. The place was magical, there were purple rivers and torrents, also 1,000ft trees with orange bark and bright yellow leaves; the place was outstanding. The seemingly malicious was beautiful.

Jack Price (11)

Ivybridge Community College, Ivybridge

A Day In The Life Of Jimmy

One sunny day Jimmy was walking to tennis.
When he got there he went on the tennis court
and won all of his matches. He went to the final
and got hit in the eye and walked back home.

James Scarr (12)
Ivybridge Community College, Ivybridge

Biggit

Biggit was a dwarf from St Ives. He had ginger hair, green eyes and blue velvet clothes. Biggit had only one friend, Tulula. She was an eleven-year-old little girl. Tulula found Biggit on the beach and decided to keep him. But Biggit died soon after.
RIP.

Holly Taylor (12)
Ivybridge Community College, Ivybridge

97

Graveyard Legend

Down at the graveyard the owls are hooting, the
cats are miaowing and the souls are screaming.
There's a legend that no one believes; at
Halloween the witch will come and light the black
flame candle, the skeletons will rise and the sky
will go black and we'll die!

Juliet Hepburn (12)
Ivybridge Community College, Ivybridge

Roller Coaster

'Here I go, a roller coaster.' I lined up for ten
minutes, I was going to do it! My first roller
coaster. My friend was nervous, I was so excited I
nearly wet myself.
I was on the coaster then I thought, *do I want to
waste my time? No!*

Luke Forward (11)
Ivybridge Community College, Ivybridge

99

Untitled

I was sitting in bed, trying to get to sleep, when I heard footsteps coming up the stairs but nobody was at home. Then I felt a gust of wind go past me. I was getting scared!
I managed to get to sleep after that. Nothing has ever happened since.

Lauren Kerr (12)

Ivybridge Community College, Ivybridge

Nowhere To Run

Night-time on the plane, gliding above the Atlantic Ocean. The plane shudders, people panic, luggage everywhere, humidity decreasing fast. Plane thrashes, sea submerging immediately, everyone unconscious, except me. I panic and attempt escape, forcing past disturbed clothes. Finally freedom, fresh air, murky surroundings, scared, alone, marooned on an island ...

Matthew Burnard (13)
Ivybridge Community College, Ivybridge

Untitled

All of a sudden, *bang!* The door slammed open
and inside the wardrobe stood a figure. 'Hello?' I
said quietly. There was no answer and the figure
vanished. *Crash!* The light bulb smashed and
everything seemed to go dead. I was alone at last
and slowly crept back into bed.

Megan Bush (11)
Ivybridge Community College, Ivybridge

Untitled

Humpty-Dumpty went to a wall; Humpty-Dumpty tripped on a ball, Humpty-Dumpty went to hospital, Humpty-Dumpty went to play with a ball and we never saw him again. Humpty-Dumpty sat on a ball, Humpty-Dumpty had another great fall.
Humpty-Dumpty went to the hospital ... again.

Jake Lockley
Ivybridge Community College, Ivybridge

Untitled

Worm lived in a garden with lots of his wormy and bug friends. When he climbed out of his small muddy burrow in the morning, none of his friends were out. The late bird never came out in the morning but one bird did and ate him.

Connor Newman (12)

Ivybridge Community College, Ivybridge

The Incy-Wincy Sheep

Incy-Wincy Sheep climbed up the rocky hill, down came the bull and took the sheep out. Up came the sheep and tried it again, got back on his legs and marched on. Once at the top it rested but not for long because the bull took him out!

Jack Brodie (11)

Ivybridge Community College, Ivybridge

105

The Day Of A Tasty Pasty

Once upon a time a tasty pasty went into the cupboard and found a cream biscuit. He then went to the shop to buy some Bourbons but before he could get to the biscuits he had a cardiac arrest in the fish aisle. He was rushed to hospital.
Very smelly!

Toby Browne (12)
Ivybridge Community College, Ivybridge

Gone

Once upon a time there was a girl called Amilia,
she lived on a farm in Devon. One day she went
walking with her dog, then she heard a scream.
She went to investigate and found out that there
was no one there.

Leigh Coleman (11)
Ivybridge Community College, Ivybridge

A Ghostly Hand And A Door

As the door creaked open, one ghostly
transparent hand, pasted with blood-red claws,
gripped the icy door handle. A sudden chill swept
over the room like a tidal wave. Shivering under
the threadbare sheets, I reached out a shaky hand
and clutched the phone. I then dialled 999 ...
Darkness!

Catherine Romney (11)
Ivybridge Community College, Ivybridge

A Restless Man

The restless man tossed and turned in his
uncomfortable bed. His eyes stretched open,
waiting for her to arrive. His heart forever racing,
the blood in his veins froze as he heard her
creeping up the stairs, muttering her madness.
Why, oh why, did he push her down the stairs?

Miriam Silsbury (15)
Ivybridge Community College, Ivybridge

The Haunted House

At midnight me and Jack went to the house in the centre of the forest. The house had been abandoned for twenty years. As we walked in, Jack fell through the floorboards. I jumped down after him. He had fallen on a spike and I landed on one after.

Toby Yeoman (15)
Ivybridge Community College, Ivybridge

Zapatos

Here I was on the planet of Zapatos, about to be
killed. The aliens looked like they hadn't washed
for a year but I didn't care because I was about to
be demolished.
Suddenly the aliens said something then one
approached me with a knife ...

Dan Burnley (12)
Ivybridge Community College, Ivybridge

The Mouse

Creep, creep. The mouse crept out of his house
and into the kitchen. He was in luck. There was
some cheese on the kitchen side. *Snatch! Gobble!*
The cheese was gone. Satisfied the mouse started
to creep back to his hole.
On no! Standing in his way was the cat ...

Jack Smerdon (11)
Ivybridge Community College, Ivybridge

Humpty-Dumpty Retold!

On the floor, by a wall, someone had a fall.
Soldiers marched past to the sound of horses'
hooves, they glanced and laughed to see in front
of them, scrambled on the floor, lay Humpty-
Dumpty.
You would not believe how tasty he was!

Rebecca Johns (11)
Ivybridge Community College, Ivybridge

113

The First Of Many!

I woke this morning to find that my wife had given me another daughter, it was wrong, I needed a son!
Two years later, inspiration struck. I had to open my own church. I soon got the divorce but from here on in, things went downhill ...
Henry VIII, 1527.

Tiegen Lillicrap (12)
Ivybridge Community College, Ivybridge

A Twist In The Tale, Twisted Stairs

She ran faster and faster down the twisted stairs. Their only chance was to reach the front door. But the girl was gaining on them, getting closer and closer by the second. They were nearly there, within touching distance of their destination.

'Got you!' Tom wished he had been faster.

Alex Griffiths (12)

Ivybridge Community College, Ivybridge

The Day

Nobody moved, no soul dared to speak. The only
unicorn in existence had come. It's blood-red skin
glinting in the bright moonlight. *Bang!* It happened
so suddenly but slowly in my mind.
It keeps me awake even now thinking back to
that memorable day ... the day my unicorn died.

Alicia Clarke (12)
Ivybridge Community College, Ivybridge

Gone

A pale silver trickle of moonlight shone through the clouds. A pair of rubies peered through the fog, a low growl made me feel as cold as if I had just fallen into a pile of snow. I heard a padding of paws getting louder, closer, then it all disappeared.

Naomi Keenan (11)
Ivybridge Community College, Ivybridge

A Twist In The Tale

Fishy swam, eager to get away from his pursuer.
He finally realised that he had swum into a trap.
His only hope was to swim although the gap was
ever smaller, but suddenly his tail was twisted - he
had no chance of escape.
Suddenly, down came a giant spear, spearing
Fishy!

Oliver Tyers (12)
Ivybridge Community College, Ivybridge

Holiday Adventures

I was walking along a cliff when, all of a sudden, it came for me. I dived for the nearest bush; I was paralysed with fear for a few seconds. The light was blinding, then I noticed the silhouette of a dragon breathing fire over the surroundings.
Or was it?

Jack Tremlett (11)
Ivybridge Community College, Ivybridge

119

Ghost

Alone, cold, dead, pale. Bleeding and tormented. Bloodshot eyes, ravaged skin, broken mind. The pain in its face. The stab wound to the heart. The grizzly step it takes towards you. An outstretched hand seals your fate. Shadows envelop your figure. Never heard from again, you have been sacrificed, *RIP* ...

Victoria James (12)

Ivybridge Community College, Ivybridge

Death's Come

I was on my way to collect the groceries from the car. I looked inside but all the groceries had gone. I was about to go back inside the house when I heard a sound. In the corner was a bloody head munching! It said, 'I am still hungry ...'

Sarah Woodyear (12)
Ivybridge Community College, Ivybridge

121

Jaffa Cakes

As the door creaked open I looked around to see nobody there. But the fridge door opened by itself. Ever so carefully I tiptoed over to the fridge and there, standing in front of me, was a big black dragon! It was eating all my Jaffa cakes!

Chloe Adams-Smith (12)

Ivybridge Community College, Ivybridge

The Death Trap

Death was everywhere. Nowhere was safe.
Cobwebs were slung everywhere, flies
smothered on them like icing on a cake.
Kathy ran on and on, she chased and chased
through all the rooms of this once grand house.
Where had it gone? Then, *bang!* Black!
And a repulsive smell ...

Alice Wigmore (11)
Ivybridge Community College, Ivybridge

123

The Shadow

The shadow flickered in the dusky light. I held
my breath, my heart stopped beating and my legs
turned to jelly. I could see his feet now. He was
wearing black shoes which made a *clack-clack*
noise when he walked.
I was scared. I held my breath and waited ...

Sarah Bone (12)

Ivybridge Community College, Ivybridge

Hunting The Hunted

His feet crunched on the gravel. He cradled his gun in his hands. The moonlight glinted on the barrel. Meanwhile Tom lay in the bushes watching. The movement caught his eye, he aimed carefully. His attacker disappeared. He walked to his friend. 'No sign of him,' he said. 'Damn it!'

William Battershill (12)

Ivybridge Community College, Ivybridge

The Loch

Don't go swimming in the bottom of a loch, especially if you don't know what's lurking down there. As Amy Fisher found out, it's not always what it seems to be. Something saw her in the depths one night and she was never seen again. That proves Nessie's not vegetarian!

Daniel Sansom (12)

Ivybridge Community College, Ivybridge

Sam And The Leprechaun

Sam went downstairs to do breakfast. Sam poured out his golden nugget and a mini leprechaun fell out. 'Leave my gold alone!' said the leprechaun.
'It's my breakfast!' said Sam but the leprechaun had taken one golden nugget from his bowl. He chased him. 'Mum! A leprechaun stole my breakfast!'

Steven Booth (10)
Lake Middle School, Isle of Wight

127

Monster In The Kitchen

All I could hear was *munch, munch, munch.*
coming from below. It had been doing it for some
time, a monster in my kitchen. I had set up CCTV
down there, so I could report it to the police.
I looked up the wire and turned it on ... *My cat!*

Sam Lapham (11)
Lake Middle School, Isle of Wight

The Avalanche

I'm climbing a mountain. *'Oops!'* I fall down, a
thunder of snow crashes down on me. Rocks hit
my poor, ugly face, *'Ow!'* My small, fearful head is
pouring out gallons of blood into a wine glass.
Suddenly, I wake up.
'That'll be ninety pence please,' says the kind
barman.

George Lawrence (10)
Lake Middle School, Isle of Wight

129

The Elevator Drama

Stephen stood as the doors opened with a bang. Suddenly, an enormous crowd wanted to get in. The doors closed with everybody talking as loud as a brass band. However, that was the least of my worries since there was a man as fat as a cheeseburger squashing me.

Max Dennes (10)
Lake Middle School, Isle of Wight

The Skydive

An old man was on a jet plane, ready to do a
skydive from 1,000 feet. He jumped. He was
falling down - then, panic. He forgot to put on
a parachute. The ground was getting closer. He
could see the grass clearly.
'Grandad, what are you doing in the garden?'

Chris Taylor (11)
Lake Middle School, Isle of Wight

131

The Mars Landing

It was an amazing sight for mankind. Police, security guards and tourists had given up their time to watch me step on Mars' surface. First foot down. I'd stepped on the huge planet.
'Get off there!' yelled the police and guards.
I was in the planetarium pretending to be famous!

Tom Lawrence (10)
Lake Middle School, Isle of Wight

Charlie, The Chicken

On a bright sunny farm, Charlie was playing with the smelly chickens. Then a tiny, fluffy baby chick hatched out of the small egg. Someone asked, laughing, 'Charlie, what are you doing?' as he was lying on the floor acting like a chicken in the middle of the chicken aisle.

George Ridgway-Bamford
Lake Middle School, Isle of Wight

My Best Friend

Harry is the bravest boy I've ever known. He is fast, intelligent and cool. He is funny and fearless. He isn't scared of anything at all. Everyone likes him! He is popular, he is my best friend. He loves food and running.
Harry is the best hamster I've ever known!

Tom Leaver (11)

Lake Middle School, Isle of Wight

The Confusion Of The Hunt

Wolf crossed the Blackpath where Man drove his
foul-smelling monsters. Loping along, he tried to
ignore the field of cows, knowing that if he killed,
Man would come with guns.
But Wolf was so hungry ... Quickly he made his
kill. A shout, a bang, and Wolf was no more ...

Abigail Plant (12)

Lake Middle School, Isle of Wight

Race

I'm nervous. I'm doing a race in front of hundreds
of people and I'm frightened. On the starting line
I feel beads of sweat dripping down my forehead
already. I've never felt this way before. I could trip
up.
The blank goes, fellow racers run and I go
sprinting. Winning!

Warren Chare (12)

Lake Middle School, Isle of Wight

The Kite

The kite soared into the crystal-blue sky. As the kite floated up towards the clouds, raindrops slowly began to fall. But the kite was not disheartened. Dodging the raindrops, which were as light as a feather, it reached the clouds waiting above. Safety, escape from the humans at last.

Abbie Tibbott (11)

Lake Middle School, Isle of Wight

Noises In The Night

It was dark, the wind howled outside and the
branches of a tree tapped my windowpane.
Among the noise of the night I could hear a faint
patter of feet coming quickly closer. I sank slowly
below the covers as the door creaked open and
in came … a mouse!

Hannah Mudge (11)
Lake Middle School, Isle of Wight

The Deep, Dark Forest

Suddenly I was in a deep, dark forest with nobody
with me. All there was, was an owl shining in the
moonlight. Plus there was silent music coming
from nowhere ...
Unexpectedly a troll came towards me out of a
shed. What was happening? Nothing!

Vincent Rankine (11)
Lake Middle School, Isle of Wight

139

Spooky Dungeon

I walk through the creepy dungeon, I hear a
spooky noise, I don't quite know what to do. I'm
all alone. *Please, someone, tell me what to do.* I
discovered this place at my friend's house. I've
just seen a shovel, a creepy man.
I realise I'm in a shed!

Peter Barfoot (11)
Lake Middle School, Isle of Wight

The Creature

It's a lovely sunny day, I'm on my daily walk but suddenly I hear something. It's coming from the bushes. So scared, I stutter, 'Hello? Hello? Is anyone there, hello?' There is another sound, I need to run, then suddenly it creeps out, it is ... a terrifying, monstrous, deadly ... cat!

Georgina Corbett (11)

Lake Middle School, Isle of Wight

141

The Target

I walk through the shopping centre seeking my
targets without being spotted. I get a message
from the boss. The man in black with the green
hat, he's my target to kill. I must stealthily kill him.
I find the security room. Taking out my sniper,
I take him out!

Luke Smith (11)

Lake Middle School, Isle of Wight

Death

I am Death. I kill everyone and everything in my path. I cause death and despair wherever I go. I separate families and destroy friendships. I am everywhere and I am nowhere. I kill the countryside and demolish cities. No one can run or hide from me. I am War!

Callum Kotsapas (12)
Lake Middle School, Isle of Wight

143

The Shadow Men

They're after me. The shadow men are after me.
I should never have come here at night.
I reach a river. I cannot jump as a monster lurks
in the murky depths. I run back. They surround
me. They take down their hoods. They are my
teachers!
'Remember your homework!'

Joshua Perfect (12)
Lake Middle School, Isle of Wight

The Sniper

I am disguised like the grass; my olive-green ghillie
suit keeps me camouflaged like a snake in the
grass. I go on, crawling around the enemy like a
predator, eliminating my prey one by one. I move
into a deserted building. There is my target.
I take the shot!

James Treherne (11)
Lake Middle School, Isle of Wight

Emily And The Sandwich

Emily, famished, was staring at her companion.
Sweat was dripping from her head, as she tried to
conquer her hunger. Time was running out, and
Emily's anxiety was growing. She had to eat it.
Ashamed of herself, she carried on eating.
Emily had lost, and her hunger was satisfied.

Marnie Hemming (12)
Lake Middle School, Isle of Wight

Mini Marvels Terrific Tales

The Sandwich

There it was. It was perfect. It looked delicious. I had to eat it. Taking a huge bite out of the perfect sandwich, I could feel my hunger disappearing. The crispiness of the bacon went perfectly with its companions.

Bella Carter (11)

Lake Middle School, Isle of Wight

147

School

I stood, staring at it, with my huge round eyes.
The door flung open. A man came out and said
loudly, 'Come on in little boy, do you know where
you should be, young child?'
'No Sir,' I replied, shivering.
'Then, welcome to our school,' said the
headmaster. 'Good luck!'

Matthew Gibbon (13)
Lake Middle School, Isle of Wight

The Mystery

Scared, I jump behind the sofa, terrified of
what's going to happen next. The phone rings,
too scared to answer it, it's left there. It's misty
outside, figures standing there. I can feel terror in
the atmosphere, I can hear laughing.
'I thought you liked scary films,' said my mum.

Georgia Rostron (12)
Lake Middle School, Isle of Wight

149

The Ghost

The dark house sat there on the hill. Only one light on ... The bedroom. The ghost floated gracefully up the hill. It moved up to the door and slowly opened it with a creak ... It moved up the stairs slowly. The lady opened the door nervously ...
'Trick or treat?'

Charlie Abbott (13)

Lake Middle School, Isle of Wight

School

I never liked school, still don't, probably never will. It's not fair, we only get thirteen weeks off a year and occasional trips. I like bossing people around though, telling them what to do. I like school ... as a teacher, that is. The poor kids suffer, that's what teaching's about!

Alice Lyons (12)
Lake Middle School, Isle of Wight

151

My Friend, Felix

My friend, Felix, is the best ever, they bully me
because of him but I don't care. He may be just a
cat but he is the only friend I have. We play hide-
and-seek but this all ended when Felix passed
away. Now I have a new dog!

Tia Ashley (12)

Lake Middle School, Isle of Wight

Ghost

Running up the stairs, hearing a bang, his breaths hard and uneven. Opening the door, his heart misses a beat. Frozen with fear, there's a cold breath on his neck. He walks a step further but it matches his step. He turns round and sees the neighbour's cat, Tom.

Kirsten Taylor (13)
Lake Middle School, Isle of Wight

Pitch-Black

The sky was pitch-black, not a cloud in the air.
I walked down the zombie-infested alleyway. I
could hear footsteps coming faster and faster
towards me. So I started sprinting, my heart
pumping as fast as it could go. I tripped. The
shadow grew. Suddenly a mouse emerged.

Arron Hunter (13)
Lake Middle School, Isle of Wight

Untitled

Happily skipping along the lane, the little blonde
girl beams with a smile across her face. The clear
sky and fresh green grass pass as she carries on.
Something rustles in the hedge. She stops. The
smile dies. It gets closer, she's backing up.
Out it jumps, the fearsome robin!

Blythe Ely (13)
Lake Middle School, Isle of Wight

The Scream

It's late, dark, cold. My family is sitting by the fire,
shivering in the dim light. I hear a loud scream, a
person attacked ... maybe?
We go outside, search the deep depths of the
underground. A figure in the darkness shaking
uncomfortably. I adjust my eyes, *'Ahh!* It's an owl.'

Max Harris (12)

Lake Middle School, Isle of Wight

Is It A Ghost?

Almost asleep, I hear a noise, it's coming from
the kitchen. *Clatter, bang, clash, crash!* It must be
a ghost. With my body shaking, I go downstairs
with a bat in my hand. I reach for the handle,
I slowly open the door and ... *Phew,* it's only
Tommy, the cat.

Rebekah Gregory (13)
Lake Middle School, Isle of Wight

Teachers Unmasked

I opened the door, *creak* ... I stepped back, slowly
I peered through. *Splash*. *'Urgh,* green slime!'
The rumours were right, teachers were ... aliens!
I decided to make a run for it. *Creak!* Forgot
about the door. They'd spotted me, I tried to run
but I couldn't move. The slime, *argh!*

Nathan Collings (12)
Lake Middle School, Isle of Wight

Untitled

Bang! The boy quietly lies in his bunker. Bombs, cannons and guns all around, fighting for life. He slowly rises, moving confidently. He then falls to the ground, taking his last breath. Of course turning back, to reality, being a boy, he gets agitated and turns off the PlayStation 3.

Jasmine Watt (12)
Lake Middle School, Isle of Wight

159

The Quest

Climbing through the air, up the mountain I go,
wind rushes through my hair, trying to dash
the rocks that fly by me. The sky is bright blue,
without a cloud. Eventually I am here, right on the
top of Mount Everest ...
'Toby, what're you doing on the floor?'

Georgia Bennett (13)
Lake Middle School, Isle of Wight

Loved-Up

I knew he loved me. Yet, this was ridiculous. He would cuddle me all the time. He was forever telling me, 'Oh I love you so much that it makes my heart ache.'
I mean seriously, this is just yucky. How many dogs are this loved-up by their owner?

Elle Garland (13)
Lake Middle School, Isle of Wight

Rain

It's raining, I'm cold and I'm wet. Home feels a
million miles away, I have no umbrella and no
coat. It's dark and I'm scared. A car pulls up
beside me, I don't think; I get in. Now I wish I'd
never, as I think this could be the end!

Jade Napper (11)

Lake Middle School, Isle of Wight

Dark Room

Stood in a dark room, Kelly was scared. Suddenly
small thumps came from above, getting louder
and louder. Then unfamiliar voices started saying,
'Where are you, Kelly? Where are you?'
Kelly got more scared as footsteps came down
the stairs. Then the bright light came on …
'*Surprise!* Happy birthday Kelly!'

Carrie-Anne Gatland (13)
Lake Middle School, Isle of Wight

163

Ghost Town With Scooby-Doo

One day Scooby-Doo and the gang went to a spooky house. They went and saw a ghost. They followed the ghost and realised they were being tricked. They set up a trap to try and catch the ghost.

After some hard attempts they caught the ghost and went home.

Benjamin Millross (13)

Maidenhill School, Stonehouse

Cheater

The sparkle in his eyes. The way I felt so special when he asked me to be his girl and then the crushing pain when I realised that he was with someone other than me.
Scott wants to go out again but the indescribable pain is just too unbearable!

Amiee Jones
Maidenhill School, Stonehouse

Pixies For Sale

'Keep running,' screamed Kacey to Emily.
The two girls ran. Bark crumpled under their
feet. Wind and rain slapped their faces. Emily
and Kacey had to keep running, they were in
complete danger. The moon shone, it gave them
light to see. It was midnight and help was gone ...
Bang!

Vanezza Avinante (13)

Maidenhill School, Stonehouse

Holiday Adventures

I entered the airport. It was the first time I had ever been on a plane. When we took off I had a rush of adrenaline. When we finally arrived at our hotel room we unpacked and then our holiday began. We went all sorts of places. It was amazing.

Molly Poole (12)
Maidenhill School, Stonehouse

Untitled

'*Wow!* Connor come in here.' *Bang!*
'Ollie, that was the door!' They both ran up to the door and with all of their might, they were trying to open it!
A voice appeared and spoke, 'You are being gassed with deadly smoke, you will die in ... *3, 2, 1, dead!'*

Kitty Rochford (13)
Maidenhill School, Stonehouse

The Dark Closet

In the depths of our school there is a dark closet
that has been made a forbidden area. Nobody
dares to enter, they fear they will never come
out. Many stories have been told, the eerie
air, the only thing still alive to enter the closet.
Nothing else has survived.

Molly Gardner (13)
Maidenhill School, Stonehouse

A Day In The Life Of Glisten The Fairy

I'm Glisten, a water fairy. I have many jobs. One time, I was helping tadpoles swim and a hawk started chasing fairies, so I threw water droplets at him. He became frightened and flew away. Nobody was hurt. Later that day the queen fairy rewarded me with a bravery medal.

Kelly Prosser (13)
Maidenhill School, Stonehouse

Henry's Wives

Henry VIII had six wives. Catherine of Aragon,
Anne Boleyn, Jane Seymour, Anne of Cleeves,
Catherine Howard and Katherine Parr. Catherine
of Aragon was divorced, Anne Boleyn was
beheaded. Jane Seymour died, Anne of Cleeves
was divorced. Catherine Howard was beheaded
and Katherine Parr survived. Henry died before
Katherine Parr.

Amber-Paige Stanley (12)
Maidenhill School, Stonehouse

The Last Look

I saw my mum and called to her. She turned
and smiled at me. I started to walk towards her.
Someone jumped out of the shadows and killed
her. I screamed and ran towards her. He went
behind me and put the knife to my throat …
Then I woke up!

Chloe Neve (13)

Maidenhill School, Stonehouse

The Relic

Adam West ventured deeper into the cavern. For years he'd been searching and now he'd found it. The Obsidian Sword! He reached out to take it and the Earth violently shook. He grabbed it and ran for the exit, dodging falling boulders. He made it out! The relic was his!

Rebecca Jones (13)
Maidenhill School, Stonehouse

173

Hansel And Gretel

Hansel and Gretel are poor. Their dad abandoned them in the woods and they left a trail of rocks and ran back home. Then their dad did it again and they found a house of sweets and a witch found them. She tried to cook them but they ran away.

Oliver Williams (12)

Maidenhill School, Stonehouse

I'm Doing This For Them

200 down, 700,000 to go. I'm doing it for them,
the people that died y'know. Everyone I kill is 100
lives saved. People respect me wherever I play,
part behind our lines or behind enemy lines. I
can't mourn my friends. War is upon us.
Till the end I fight.

Blake Squibb (13)

Maidenhill School, Stonehouse

175

The Shot Of Truth

Agent James was right outside the doors that held
him from his target. He jacked the CCTV with his
computer. He entered. There he stood, Viosky,
the Mastermind. The shot was hard but James
made it. Word of the assassination spread quickly.
James was surrounded, *bang!* To be continued ...

James Lapidge (12)

Maidenhill School, Stonehouse

176

Mini Marvels Terrific Tales

The War On The Philippine Islands

In late 1944 the Americans started an invasion
on the Philippine islands. The Japanese had set
up bunkers on top of the hill. The Americans
pushed up the hill with casualties but took out
the bunkers with flame-throwers. The Japanese
surrendered to the Americans.

Ryan Jones (13)

Maidenhill School, Stonehouse

Holiday Adventures

There were two girls called Rosie and Hannah
and they went on an adventure to find treasure.
They found a treasure map on the path and they
went to find it on the beach. They found the spot
and started digging. But they didn't find anything
and they were disappointed.

Sophie Alice Berry (12)
Maidenhill School, Stonehouse

Bandit

Bandit stood in the kitchen, he was looking, he was looking for lunch. Bandit went over to his bowl, it wasn't there, where had his owners put it? He saw my lunchbox! Bandit ate the contents. When we arrived back home, Bandit wasn't in the kitchen, but fast asleep.

Reece Allen (13)
Maidenhill School, Stonehouse

The Dangerous Dare

One day Kyle and Luke played dares. Luke did
his dare then told Kyle to do his. Kyle wasn't
quick enough and got hit by the car. Luke phoned
the ambulance - Kyle was taken to hospital but,
luckily, only suffered scratches and bruises.
Kyle never did dares after that.

Kyle King (12)
Maidenhill School, Stonehouse

The Big Wave

I was guarding Borth beach. The radio said a big
surge would hit Borth in seconds. Lifeguards
evacuated everyone. When I saw the enormous
wave I froze it before it broke. When the ice
melted I dived to find the rocks rubbing together.
I moved them away. Nathan saved Borth.

Nathan Heaven (13)

Maidenhill School, Stonehouse

Rapunzel

When the prince heard about Rapunzel he went
to where she was said to be locked up. He
called, 'Rapunzel, Rapunzel, let down your hair!'
Rapunzel did. He climbed. When he got to the
top Rapunzel dashed through the open door and
locked it.
The prince watched Rapunzel run off.

Willow Driversharp (12)
Maidenhill School, Stonehouse

Ghostly Mystery

Alice climbed slowly into bed, she lay down in silence. *Tap, tap, tap.* 'What's that?' She scanned the room carefully. Nothing! *Crash!* She sat up and climbed out of bed, walked to the bathroom where the sound was coming from. She opened the door. *Tap, tap, tap!* Just some water.

Amelia Ribbens (12)

Maidenhill School, Stonehouse

183

Bang! A Shot From A Single Gun Kills Somebody!

Bill and John were talking then, *bang!* Gunshots! They ran like bullets but Bill had been attacked by the shot. John ran home to get help then a bullet shot past his head, just skimming it. He hid as a white figure shot past him then Bill was dead.

Curtis Woods (12)

Maidenhill School, Stonehouse

Some Holiday!

Mum, Dad and Ellie are going on holiday. Dad clumsily drives into a lamp post. Mum, Dad and Ellie get out the car. Dad tries to fix the car but ends up getting his head trapped. They search for a nearby house. They eventually find one but they get captured.

Courtney Chapman (13)
Maidenhill School, Stonehouse

The Boy Called Bobster

One day there was a boy called Bobster and he wanted to see the world. So he decided to get a train then another train but he got lost so he caught a train then another train, then two buses and got home very sadly but said he was fine.

Elle Chandler (12)

Maidenhill School, Stonehouse

Midnight Diaries

The door creaked open. I saw shadows around
my head, someone was here with me. As I looked
for that person, someone jumped out of the
darkness and grabbed me. I tried to wrestle them
off me but they were too strong. He had bitten
me. What would happen now?

Hollie Taylor (12)

Maidenhill School, Stonehouse

Mr Nosey

One day Mr Nosey was walking along the street
when he heard a scream. Right away, Nosey
looked in a hole in a fence, it was a little girl stuck
in the fence so Nosey climbed over and helped
her
Ever since, Nosey has been a hero, not Mr Nosey.

Georgia Cox (13)
Maidenhill School, Stonehouse

Humpty

Humpty was very kind. He didn't have many friends, he got bullied a lot as well! One day he was sitting on a wall by himself, he got pushed off! His heart gave up on him! Unfortunately the hospital couldn't revive him, and so nobody knew who pushed poor Humpty.

Georgina Lucarotti (13)
Maidenhill School, Stonehouse

189

The Holiday

I was going on a holiday near the beach. We went shopping. Dad and Dave went to a shop. Me and Mum went to a tourist shop. A bracelet caught my eye. Then Mum went. I couldn't find her, I walked around and found her in a shop next door.

Natasha Webb (13)

Maidenhill School, Stonehouse

Getting Into The Wrong Crowd!

'John! Do it!' yelled Kane. John was a shy boy (he
got into the wrong crowd). Kane shouted for
him to do it! John snatched the chocolate bar, he
bumped straight into a policeman. The policeman
questioned him. John got let off. But he got a
strict warning!

Courtney Cox (13)
Maidenhill School, Stonehouse

191

Escape

Bring, bring!
'Someone has escaped. Let's get a search party
on him!'
'There he is, chase him, now we still have sight of
him.'
I'm getting closer ... 'Got ya. Now let's get you
back to the prison.'
'It wasn't me, I swear, it was a man called
Jim Bob.'

Curtis Florek (9)
Maidenhill School, Stonehouse

Easter Bunny And Doc Hudson

In a cinema, people watching a movie. Suddenly a
bunny head appears. Soon blood is everywhere.
People scream and run out. The policeman's wife
is crushed to death. The policeman shoots the
Easter bunny and calls for back-up.
Doc Hudson sneaks in and takes the bunny back
to his lab ...

Caleb Lusty (13)
Maidenhill School, Stonehouse

193

Untitled

They fight and argue then they go to the death.
'You're gonna die,' says James, so they fight. Steve
punches him. He's been knocked out. Steve
throws him into the lake, he runs away and gets
away with it. James is dumped in the lake forever.

Adam Gardiner (12)

Maidenhill School, Stonehouse

Six Steps To A Girl

Luke falls in love with a girl called Eve, she's going out with Ben but soon she feels the same. They go out. Ben finds out and beats Luke up. He spots his friend kissing his sister. Eve breaks up with Ben so she can be with Luke McEnzil.

Millie Gardiner (12)

Maidenhill School, Stonehouse

Bites

As I came out of the restaurant I saw a shadow but nobody was there. I carried on walking. I turned around to see nobody there. Suddenly I felt a tingle on my neck and the next thing I knew I was on the floor with blood everywhere!

Chloe Hornsby (13)

Maidenhill School, Stonehouse

Untitled

I loved holidays and I loved adventures so I
decided to go on a holiday adventure in Spain. I
swam in the lakes under waterfalls, over rocks
and through sandcastles. It was very sunny and
fun.
I had a very close friend with me called
Ryan Hampson Jnr 2nd.

Mikey Williams
Maidenhill School, Stonehouse

197

Where's Jenna?

Boom! The window exploded out, struck the car, glass everywhere. He opened his car door, grabbed Jenna and pulled her in. Gunshots flew past them. Wheels screeched as Torrert tried to catch them. He wanted the love of his life back. Roman and Jenna drove off into the sunset.

Phillip Aylmer (13)
Maidenhill School, Stonehouse

The Ending

There were two girls and one boy. They all went into a house and they heard some strange noises coming from the basement. The girls went down and never came back up. The boy went down to check it out and none of them were ever found again.

Abigail Rickards (12)

Maidenhill School, Stonehouse

199

My Little Elf!

One day there was a girl called Lilly and she
wanted a pet but her parents wouldn't get her a
cat or dog so she went for a walk in the woods
and came across an elf called Bob. Then the elf
followed her home. 'Mum, can I keep him?'

Bronya Bagnall (12)
Maidenhill School, Stonehouse

At The Airport

My hand luggage has just gone through the machine. *Beep!* They find nail varnish. Then I walk to board the aeroplane and I get stopped. They think I am a thief.

After some arguing they let me go. Eventually I am on the aeroplane and go into a gentle sleep.

Dani Sharpe (12)
Maidenhill School, Stonehouse

201

My Holiday Adventure

We set off on a boat trip to see the coastal caves of Lagos, the trip was fantastic until the boat broke down. We started to drift out to sea. I was scared, the burly captain spoke no English. We didn't know what was happening.
Eventually another boat towed us back.

Joshua Stanton (13)

Maidenhill School, Stonehouse

Untitled

Three pigs built houses. One out of straw. A wolf blew it down. Pig ended up as a bacon butty. Next pig built it out of wood. Wolf came and blew it down. Pig ended up a sausage sandwich. Last pig used stone. Wolf couldn't blow it down and died.

Tom Jarman (12)

Maidenhill School, Stonehouse

203

Trouble In The Ocean

I was there in the depths of the ocean. It came
closer and closer. *Bang!* It smashed right through
my cage, it was there right in front of me.
It was the huge great white known for several
attacks and no one had survived any attacks …

Ethan Perry (11)
Queen Elizabeth II High School, Peel

The Bouncy Apple

The dinner bell rang. We all met in the atrium for dinner. There was me, Eryn, Harry, Brandon, Kelley, Clio and Danny. Eryn didn't want her apple so she threw it back in her lunch box. It bounced out! Everyone started laughing and couldn't stop. I cried with laughter!

Danni Callin (12)
Queen Elizabeth II High School, Peel

Ducky Goes Fishing

One lovely morning my friend, Ducky, was plodding along the gravelly road at the pace of a snail. I asked Ducky, 'Where are you going? Why are you walking so slowly?'
He said, 'Because I am going fishing but the nice fish don't come out till 5am and it's 4.45am.'

Chloe Shimmin (12)

Queen Elizabeth II High School, Peel

No Way Out

Crash! Nine people, including a baby, jolted forward. An elderly man fell on the cold, smooth floor and a young lady with spiky hair, wearing an iPod, helped pick him up. 'Thank you,' he smiled. 'S'no probs,' she answered, looking around the confined space to make sure everybody was okay.

Chelsey Kneen (12)
Queen Elizabeth II High School, Peel

I'm Dying

My mum shouted me for dinner. 'I can't Mum,
I'm dying!'
My mum rushed upstairs, 'Are you OK?' she cried.
'Yes Mum, I'm playing New Super Mario Bros on
Wii! That stupid piranha plant keeps throwing
fireballs at me! Plus, I'm nearly at the finish!'
Then I died, again!

Chloe Convery (11)
Queen Elizabeth II High School, Peel

Katie Price Is Dead

'Hi, I am Katie Price's mum. Three years ago today Katie went to the Isle of Man, she went to Crosby post office and sadly got murdered by a hairy fishmonger! At first we didn't know why but we do now, thanks to PC Sheephead. We will miss her loads!'

Caitlin Hume

Queen Elizabeth II High School, Peel

The Super Scuba-Diver!

One day, on a boat near the Great Barrier Reef in Australia, a boy named James was getting ready to go scuba-diving with his dad. When they hopped into the cold blue water James felt a chill. They saw loads of fish like tuna, salmon, cod and many more.

Danny Shefford (11)

Queen Elizabeth II High School, Peel

The Big Fish

Bob went on walking up the cliff and saw a great big white shark jump out of the water going for a fish. The fish had the advantage. The fish had agility and speed. This fish was quite big. The shark had gone so I caught the big fish.

Simon Sheath (11)
Queen Elizabeth II High School, Peel

211

Toyshop

As I walked through the toyshop all the magnificent toys shone at me. I felt in a completely different world - all the beautiful colours and expensive toys that I would like to buy and share with my friends. Only trouble was it was the middle of a credit crunch.

Ryan Bibby (11)
Queen Elizabeth II High School, Peel

Toyshop

Here it stands, staring at me with its dazzling plastic eyes through the shop window. I have saved my pocket money for the last year for this wooden soldier. My steps of triumph walk towards the shop door. *Slam!* I freeze and fall to the ground in despair. 'It's closed!'

Greg Kelly (11)
Queen Elizabeth II High School, Peel

Cold Air

One lovely evening, me and my friend went out
for a jog. The sweat on my head poured down
my face like water.
Suddenly everything went quiet and the air got
cold. Something big and black jumped out at me
and carried me off into the dark, creepy forest ...

Emily Smith (11)
Queen Elizabeth II High School, Peel

Cinderella Fella

The stepsisters were challenging me to try the
shoe on. No good! My tiny feet were exploring
inside the roomy shoe. The stepsisters cackled.
Their wart-coated, 'perfect' sized feet fitted like
a glove. They linked arms with the handsome
prince.
I was left with my tutting godmother.

Leena Anwar (12)

Queen Elizabeth II High School, Peel

215

White Horses

'*Ooh*, a nice beach,' Rose said joyfully to herself. It was a bright, hot, sunny day and the waves were bursting with joy. Speaking of waves; 'Oh those majestic white horses are beautiful,' gasped Rose. 'Yes, yes, they are,' the rock added. '*Argh!*' Rose screamed, 'who are all of you?'

Megan Greggor (11)
Queen Elizabeth II High School, Peel

Mini Marvels Terrific Tales

The Terrifying Crocodile

The crocodile silently lurked through the dark
depths of the stream, waiting for its prey to
arrive. A buffalo wanted to get to its herd.
Zoom! The buffalo went for it, the crocodile
burst from the water and grabbed the buffalo.
The buffalo kicked the crocodile. The buffalo had
won.

Sean Drewry (11)
Queen Elizabeth II High School, Peel

217

The Butterflies

An illusion of dazzling indigo, yellow, pink and red
fluttered past in a multicoloured rainbow. I stood
there in the golden sunlight, gazing in awe at them
dancing in all their glory. I listened to the birds
chirping to one another. It was all so magical,
my heart fluttered.

Meggen McCann (11)

Queen Elizabeth II High School, Peel

Flying Castle Inn

One day I was walking down the road with some mates, we were going to the Flying Castle Inn. When we got there the place was a wreck. Suddenly the bartender ran outside. 'There's a huge two-headed bear with rabies!' We got Timmy's shotgun and saved the day.

Juan Joughin (12)
Queen Elizabeth II High School, Peel

219

The Man

He looked gaunt, tired, bloodshot eyes, his shirt
was ripped, blood splattered down the front, split
lip, staggering along the pavement. Every sound
was like a rumble of thunder rolling in his head.
Children walking past on their way to school,
pointing, laughing … Just another night on the
town …

Laura Davison (15)
St Sampson's High School, Guernsey

The Hunt Of Darkness

There I was, cowering in the darkness. The
hunt had begun. There, the clattering of hooves
coming closer and closer until … there! At the
end of the cobbled street, movement in the
shadows. They'd arrived. Done for. The last thing
I heard was my blood-curdling scream and a
woman's shriek.

Elicia Upson (11)
St Sampson's High School, Guernsey

221

John, The Pig

There once was a pig called John, he liked to go to feasts. Once he got invited to one and they put him in a cooking pot. He got out and they chased him and then one got a blowtorch out and cooked him brown and ate him up.

Jed Ferbrache
St Sampson's High School, Guernsey

The Hero

There once was a legend called James. He was a soldier. One day he was in a battle. All of his men died and he was the only person left on his team. There were 250 of the enemies left. Then he eventually defeated the enemies and became a hero.

Charlie Roger (12)
St Sampson's High School, Guernsey

The Quick Duel

Out of a forest came a white-feathered griffin and a golden warrior, in a fight for salvation. The golden warrior had an energy generated spear which he aimed at the griffin's head. The griffin leapt at the warrior hungrily … The warrior quickly threw the spear into the griffin's head.

Ross Reynolds (11)

St Sampson's High School, Guernsey

The Knight's Sword

I am stroking my sword as if it were a cat or a dog, it will never leave me or betray me. My best friend, the only one who will stand by me in a fight. A true friend who gives their life just to save mine. The knight's sword.

Jake Reynolds (11)
St Sampson's High School, Guernsey

225

The Bird And The Snail

One fine day when I was a snail I was slithering around and I saw this big shadow and I got very frightened. It got bigger and bigger and closer and closer and then all of a sudden it was an orange, tiny bird and I was scared of that.

Bethany Nicholson (11)
St Sampson's High School, Guernsey

Dog Splat

A family of dogs were in their house and their owner had just finished mopping the house. But they didn't know that so they came in. The leader strutted her stuff but then all of a sudden she slipped up and all the other dogs sat there laughing and giggling.

Elisha Sealley (12)
St Sampson's High School, Guernsey

Mystery Mayhem

It was a sunny Sunday at the football. He was one of 34,000 at the game and one of 57 in the queue. He asked for a bacon burger. The owner went out back. Jack heard a bang. He went to investigate and saw the pig's gun. Owner was dead.

Jordon Martel (13)
St Sampson's High School, Guernsey

Night Of Terror

He stood rooted to the spot. He knew soon they would come, unstoppable. His breathing was ragged and heavy. He could see them now. They were on the street! A crowd of ghosts, zombies and witches.

There was a knock at the door. Slowly, the door opened.

'Trick or treat?'

Callum Tostevin-Hall (11)

St Sampson's High School, Guernsey

229

Cold-Hearted Attack

He was caught in the open, in sight of the enemy. His friend watched in horror as they lined up their shot. The friend stood in front of him, ready to sacrifice himself. The deadly projectile flew through the air and then … the snowball hit him flat in the face.

Callum Conroy (15)

St Sampson's High School, Guernsey

The Pig

The pig runs and rolls in his mud unaware of his
fate. Once he's all grown up, lovely, big and juicy
he will be ready and seasoned for a big Christmas
meal. He will cook in the oven at 200° for three
hours and then he will be for dinner.

Chris Gavey (13)
St Sampson's High School, Guernsey

231

The Swim

A fish alone in silence. A crocodile is waiting to strike - he streams alone, chasing and snapping for his feast. He spots a bigger fish that's after the crocodile, the fish is safe but the crocodile is gone - bones left behind, a trail in the sea, a crocodile no more.

Jason Hodge (12)
St Sampson's High School, Guernsey

The Haunted Ghost Will Come Again

The ghost returns to the haunted house as the
windows and doors creak and the dusk air kills.
The moon turns full as the wolves come out, for
the haunt of the ghost will appear again, again. As
the moon comes the third phantom will die. Love
will never appear.

Sabrina Stoddart (11)
St Sampson's High School, Guernsey

233

Bite Of The Night

In the eye of the moon, glows the graveyard.
Home to a grave, home to a vampire. Rising from
the death-infested ground, snarls at a mourner, a
maiden of 15. He bares his fangs, he pounces, and
… silence! The maiden falls, neck pierced. Ending
today's: Bite of the night.

Megan Ridley (12)
St Sampson's High School, Guernsey

234

The Life And Wives Of Henry VIII

I have had five wives, not one right for me. First divorced, second beheaded, third was perfect but died, fourth divorced again, fifth beheaded, but what is this I see heading towards me? A perfect maid for me and then the day came for my death and she lived on.

Lydia Trow (11)

St Sampson's High School, Guernsey

235

Moonlight

I was walking through the forest then the moonlight shone on my eyes. Then a cat ran around me and ran off and I fell down a hole. I tried to get out, I fell back in it. I shouted for help, nobody came to help me. At night, alone.

Nicholas Duquemin (11)

St Sampson's High School, Guernsey

Who Was That?

I went to the church that night, there was a thick fog lingering in the air. I walked around the church to my brother's gravestone, only to find it was gone. I started to walk back, I heard footsteps behind me. 'Who's that?' Whoever it was had now gone.

Ceisha Martin (11)

St Sampson's High School, Guernsey

237

Nightmare

My brain, *argh!* My head feels like it's got pins stuck inside. The lights are fading, the darkness is coming. The man in front is turning into a hideous beast, my powers are coming back, my magic turns the lights back on and my worst nightmare is real!

Kieran Grantham (13)

St Sampson's High School, Guernsey

Cat And Mouse

The cat watches his prey as it runs in and out of
the hole in the wall. Staying still, not making a
single sound while working out when to pounce
onto it. Tummy rumbling and his mouth watering
with hunger, he counts down … three, two, one
… the end of mouse.

Chloe Gavey (13)
St Sampson's High School, Guernsey

The Victory

I sprinted. The wind passed through my hair. I could not hear a thing although the crowd was cheering me on. My arms were moving up and down, up and down until I passed the line. I won! I won the race. The crowd chanted my name, 'Chloe! Chloe! Chloe!'

Chloe Sarre (12)

St Sampson's High School, Guernsey

A Very Strange Dream

It was just a normal day, the sun was up, but I was
in a very strange place made of milk chocolate,
but every ten seconds it turned into rock. I went,
'What?' and then I realised I had no clothes on.
Then I woke up and felt very happy.

Antonio Strappini (12)
St Sampson's High School, Guernsey

241

The Forest

One day there was a swing in the big black forest but below it was a monster. So two children got a sword and they went to the black forest and they waited until sunrise and they then got the sword and they killed the monster in the woods.

Nicholas Bougourd (11)

St Sampson's High School, Guernsey

The Elephant And The Big Panic

The elephant trampled through the town causing
devastation. All the people were getting scared.
'Oh no, it can't be!'
'Yes it is, it is the cops with animal aid.'
The elephant got scared and started to panic,
they tried to calm it down by throwing a big net
over it.

Stephen Reynolds (12)
St Sampson's High School, Guernsey

243

Life On The Other Side

1919. An ocean of poppies grew in the field. A girl skipped past. A petal floated into her hand. She stared. A tear dropped. 'I will never forget you Father. One day we will meet again, I just know it!' She gently closed her hand, smiled and simply skipped away.

Alisha Le Sauvage (12)

St Sampson's High School, Guernsey

The Black Beauty

She swished and shook her beautiful hair, dancing
round the ring. She ran. She walked. She jogged
and she sprinted. She pranced, jumped and got
full marks. She was first place over all the rest.
The judges said she was a lovely horse and a real
black beauty.

Chloe Sargent (12)
St Sampson's High School, Guernsey

The Evil Shadow

As I crept down the stairs I looked round the corner. I peered round the fridge, I looked behind the sofa. I saw cobwebs with spiders and rotting flies. But where was that thing? The thing that comes out every night. I need to find it … My brother!

Megan Wilson (12)

St Sampson's High School, Guernsey

The Lion And The Mouse

The jungle was scorching hot. The lion roared, he was furious. Men had trapped him in the net. A tiny mouse strolled from the jungle and examined the lion. The tiny mouse made a large hole in the net. With a roar, the lion was free, the men ran away.

Max Everitt (12)

St Sampson's High School, Guernsey

Ahoy!

The cannons pounding in the background, swords ringing in mortal combat! Gunshots galore! The fierce winds whistle past the sails! The ship rocks violently as the waves smash against the sharp wooden bow! Suddenly a devastating whirlpool appears and our ship goes down ... *Who pulled out the plug?*

Joshua Ozanne (12)

St Sampson's High School, Guernsey

Bert The Egg And His Colourful Adventures

Hi, I'm Bert and I'm an egg. I live in a box with my brothers in the fridge. One day our owner got us out and put us on the side. She was about to fry us so my brothers escaped but I stayed and she painted me pretty colours.

Jenna Sangan (11)

St Sampson's High School, Guernsey

Cheese Land!

I was in my dream place, Cheese Land!
Anything could happen. I just wanted to eat it
all but someone had already done that for me.
Disappointed, I walked in a garden and there it
was; Cheddar, Edam, *wow, Heaven!* I dived in and
had a feast fit for mice.

Bethany Hobson (11)
St Sampson's High School, Guernsey

Why Me?

Jimbob's dad wants him to go to war. Jimbob
plays with SpongeBob figures. His hair's pink.
Jimbob's not liked. He wonders why. He thinks
his hair is cool. He asks his friend, 'Why don't you
like me?'
'Because you're weird.'
'I hate you!'
His friend slapped him. He ran off.

Josh Hunter (12)
St Sampson's High School, Guernsey

251

Surprise!

On my 12th birthday I wanted a laptop and if I
want something, I get it. I went home and said,
'Mum, can I have a laptop?'
'Where am I going to get the money from? Save
up, buy it yourself. Look, here's 50p.'
'Thanks Mum, just £250 to go!'

Tyler Dodd (12)
St Sampson's High School, Guernsey

Happy Ending

Once there was a she-wolf in a house. She had to
go to the river to pick flowers. She fell in and got
wet, so her mum came. 'Where are the flowers?'
'They fell in with me, sorry they're wet.'
'OK, let's go and make a cake for tea.'

Kathy Watson (12)
St Sampson's High School, Guernsey

253

The Strange Surroundings

As the strange machine moved, we swirled and hit the side of it then through a dark place - I'm handed to another thing who pushed me along through this red line. The other thing said, 'Carton of eggs, £1.29 please … OK please come again, don't forget your receipt.'
'OK thanks.'

Scott Edwards (11)
St Sampson's High School, Guernsey

Untitled

'Quick! Run, run Molly, he's coming, he's catching up on us.'
'Come on, we have to get there. Connie, he's catching up, I don't think we are going to make it.'
We got there with seconds to go, we were at the old rickety bus stop when the 3A came.

Jodie Moore (12)
St Sampson's High School, Guernsey

255

Park Ghost Noises

Amy and I were in the park yesterday night. We kept hearing noises; they were like ghost noises, only worse. Amy and I were scared to death. *'Argh!'* We heard rustling in the bushes. 'It's scaring me! It's coming, *Argh!'* It ran out. *'Argh!'* It was just a cat!

Courtney Forman (11)
St Sampson's High School, Guernsey

The Bully!

I was bullied at school. It was the worst time of my life. I wanted to tell Mum. She was always too busy with her new job. I got home from school, called my friend then tried to tell Mum again. She heard me. She rang the school. We moved.

Kayleigh Lythgoe (11)
St Sampson's High School, Guernsey

Battle Cry

He was rushing towards the enemy on his horse,
with his sword in hand, shrieking his battle cry.
He had his shield, all battered and tatty. He wasn't
sure if he was going to make it!
'That's all for tonight Jonny.'
'Maybe we can read it tomorrow night.'
'Good night.'

Tom De La Rue (12)
St Sampson's High School, Guernsey

The Laptop

I'm just sat here, alone. So many lights, so much noise. People look at me, test me, play with me. Why don't they pick me instead of the others? I'm just as good. I've got it all; looks, colours, the lot! Finally someone's chosen me in black. I'm a Dell!

Alexander French (11)

St Sampson's High School, Guernsey

259

Food Wars

They could smell him from a mile away. His weapon glimmered in the light. 'Hold back, men. Take aim. Fire your weapons … *now!*'
'Yes Sir!'
The soldiers took aim and fired, the missiles blocking out all of the light. He raised his weapon and …
'James! Stop playing with your food!'

David Brehaut (11)
St Sampson's High School, Guernsey

Crispy Bacon

As I walked down the road I saw a shadow move.
It was Peppa Pig and Daddy Pig, they wanted
some bacon so I said, 'Turn cannibal and eat each
other,' so they did. I walked away with two pigs
worth of bacon and a gory thriller movie.

Jordan Hughes (12)
St Sampson's High School, Guernsey

The Night

The cold dark night sent a shiver through my spine. He was stood there in the moonlight. His skin was shimmering like glitter and he was as still as a statue. I was mesmerised, captured in his gaze. He drew a deep breath, hardly moved and vanished into the night.

Leanne Oliver (15)

St Sampson's High School, Guernsey

The Best Race Ever

It was the best race ever. I was in first place with only one lap to go. I was leading over Michael Schumacher who was about three and a half seconds back. I had nearly won, only 100 metres left. I was so close and then my computer froze!

Connor Rabey

St Sampson's High School, Guernsey

263

The Black Knight

The sound of horses' footsteps scars the bloodstained floors and the sound of armour clanking echoes on the battlefield. The ghost of the black knight creeps along the floorboards in a faraway tower and its spirit lurks in the souls of those who even dare to challenge it.

Robert De La Rue (11)
St Sampson's High School, Guernsey

264

The Girl Who Cried Crocodile

The girl was scared of a crocodile that she had seen. One day she cried out, 'Crocodile!' and the men came running.
She said, 'Ha-ha, I fooled you!' and off they went. She did this several times.
Until one day a crocodile came. She screamed and it ate her!

Sadie Callister
St Sampson's High School, Guernsey

Untitled

The dog was Jim. He ate cat food. Jim went out at night, I didn't know how but Jim ran freely. He didn't like going for walks, and he could climb up trees. A car hit Jim. I was told he was a cat, should have gone to Specsavers sooner.

Adam Ashcroft (12)

St Sampson's High School, Guernsey

Fire!

'Mum!' I screamed, tears streaming down my face. Luckily I managed to escape. But Mum was getting my brother. *Where is she?* Two policemen holding me back, me biting, kicking, scratching. Fire escaping from windows and doors. Surrounded by darkness, lit by the faint, flickering flames. Is my mum dead?

Georgia Denziloe (12)
St Sampson's High School, Guernsey

The Angel In The Meadow

There she sits, clear as day, in the meadow. The sun shines down and dances on her beautiful golden curls. Her angelic face holds a soft smile to perfection. She slowly fades away into the distant lands beyond ours. We only wish they could stay, but the angels never can.

Christina McColl (15)
St Sampson's High School, Guernsey

My Mum

I was running as fast as I could. It was coming for me, the most scary one of all. It was so close I could feel it breathing down my back, shouting, 'Stop! Stop! Stop!'
Just as I was getting away it grabbed me. My mum wanted a kiss!

Jack Stevenson (12)
St Sampson's High School, Guernsey

The Great Titanic

Once there was a ship, the greatest ship of all times. It was huge! With great facilities with everything you could ever think of to keep you entertained. It was the most popular ship of all ships. It really was truly amazing. They said it was unsinkable … It sank.

Enya Bessin (12)
St Sampson's High School, Guernsey

The Noise

I heard a noise coming from my room. I went up to the door. It swung open. I walked in, looking all around my room. I could not figure out what had made the noise. Then I saw what it was - my hamster running around my room. My silly hamster!

Chloe Powell (12)

St Sampson's High School, Guernsey

The Silence

I was lying in the same position for hours waiting for that one perfect shot. I was in the SAS sniper team, the adrenalin was rushing through my body as I saw the enemy captain in my sights. I scoped in on his head then the Internet went!

Connor Gaudion (14)

St Sampson's High School, Guernsey

The Weird Man

She pulled the covers over him and said, 'Sleep tight.' She then pulled the door shut.
He whimpered and said, 'I know you're there.'
A weird voice spoke out saying, 'Yes I am.' Red eyes peeped out from the wardrobe with sharp white teeth. It jumped at him. He awoke!

Scott Alexander (12)
St Sampson's High School, Guernsey

Never Buy Chips And Leave The Ketchup Behind!

I was running. The man was catching up. Blood was in his hands. He caught up. Then finally he grabbed me, I fell to the ground. I looked up. He said, 'You left your ketchup behind, that costs 20p please.'
'Oh okay then, but my chips are squished.'

Aaron Slattery (12)

St Sampson's High School, Guernsey

Nightmare

I was sitting in bed, terrified of the noises that came from everywhere, every corner, every direction, up, down, left, right, outside, inside, next door. The rooms around my room, my room. It got louder and louder then Bob, my dad, came in and said, 'Hi, wake up!'

Charlotte Cooper (13)
St Sampson's High School, Guernsey

Untitled

As the sharp blade slowly slices through me I can
feel myself tearing in two. Soon I will be in pieces
with glue being wiped on my delicate surface.
Stuck into books I will be, nobody cares. I wish I
could be with my friends as we were so close.

Storm Wilson (13)

St Sampson's High School, Guernsey

Untitled

In the middle of nowhere I heard voices. Lost
with no way out I ran. Anywhere would do. As I
flew round the corner I saw a shadow of a lion.
Panicking I tripped. I saw it getting closer. It took
an almighty leap. A mouse landed on my chest.

Josh Bright (12)

Sheldon School, Chippenham

Untitled

Dave was running, there was someone following him. He appeared onto the main street. Yes, definitely someone behind him. He dipped, darted and dashed through the people. Dave snuck into an alley. A dead end. He turned round, he cowered in the corner scared.
'Hey mate, you dropped your wallet.'

Benjamin Knowlden (12)
Sheldon School, Chippenham

The Beast!

The two men peered through the long grass, looking through their binoculars. Suddenly a large fierce-looking creature glared at them through its glassy eyes. The man froze, heart pounding, not knowing what to do. Then it sprang forward. The other man screamed, shouting, 'Argh! A mouse! Get it off!'

Hugh Seagar (12)
Sheldon School, Chippenham

Stand And Deliver

Martin was walking down a street in a happy dream. Suddenly a man jumped out at him, 'Your money or your life?' he whispered. Martin was petrified. He jumped back in fright, staring at his evil face. The man's face softened. 'Don't worry son, I am collecting for Cancer Research.'

Amelia Cox (12)

Sheldon School, Chippenham

The Unknown

Eight o'clock, pitch-black, the thick fog surrounding me. The moonlight reflecting off the dark murky water. Chris stumbled cluelessly having found his way into a forgotten, unknown swamp, in search of a body that was supposed to be around this area. As he was searching, he turned then, *whack!*

Caleb Parker (13)

Sheldon School, Chippenham

281

The Cave

The man entered the cave which was damp, dark and dingy. He progressed on through ragged terrain, the further he went, the bigger the stench. He looked back and saw horrible rotten bodies toppled onto each other. He turned forward, a figure stood motionless in the dark and murky distance.

Louis Bishop (14)

Sheldon School, Chippenham

Frederick And The Dog

Frederick was a small ebony kitten who was in a fight for survival. His family had been captured by savage Bruno, the dog. Suddenly Frederick darted at the cage his family were in. The creature leapt after him. Succeeding, he saved his family; thunderous Bruno was smashed in behind him.

Annabel Brunt

Sheldon School, Chippenham

283

Untitled

'Argh!' What was it? Who was it? Where was it coming from? 'Argh!' There it was again. But this time, louder. It was getting closer, closer and closer. It was so dark and gloomy in the deep, dark cave. Then something pounced on me with dark, red, staring eyes …

Joseph Sanderson
Sheldon School, Chippenham

Untitled

It was a dark and stormy night and a robot called Jigsaw stared into a window. It gradually got closer and closer then suddenly *bang!* He blasts through the window and shoots this boy. Blood was all over the walls and Jigsaw ate this boy, partially alive and partially dead.

Adam Mitchell
Sheldon School, Chippenham

The Wilbing Forest

Once upon a time in the Forest of Wilbing, there was a little girl happily strolling through. She heard a noise and figured it was thick branches hitting each other. She carried on walking and heard another noise. She started to get scared, she turned to find squirrels collecting nuts.

Kelsey Hamblin (13)
Sheldon School, Chippenham

The Sleepover That Came True

Once at a house there was a group of teens and they were having a sleepover and one of the girls thought it would be a good idea to tell a horror story. After telling everyone the gory, scary details it ended up being a very true story!

Lois Jenkins (13)

Sheldon School, Chippenham

Untitled

Jasmin was walking down a dark and gloomy alley. It was about 12:30 in the morning. She was only halfway through the alley when she heard heavy footsteps approaching. When suddenly she felt a hand on her shoulder, she started to panic. 'Excuse me, Miss, you dropped your phone.'

Deanna Taylor (13)
Sheldon School, Chippenham

Kidnapped

Jimmy was in his living room watching TV when his friends called him out to play. He went out to play tag. It was his turn to be the tagger. Suddenly, out of nowhere, a group of mini, evil ninjas kidnapped everyone and took them to a different dimension.

Ben Atkinson (13)
Sheldon School, Chippenham

The Alleyway

Cautiously a man was creeping down a dark abandoned alleyway. He heard a rustle from behind him and quickly turned around to find nothing. He kept on walking and it happened again but nothing was there. Now the man started to run before attacking this guy and nicking his money.

Jack Evans (12)

Sheldon School, Chippenham

Freedom

I am trapped in a bubble of summer. This is the only time in my life I have felt completely free. The freedom is rushing through my body as I walk through the fields. If someone was to see me now, they would notice no difference, for love is invisible!

Lucie Horton (16)
Sheldon School, Chippenham

291

Murdered

There was a horrible old man who lived next door to this lady. He was old with blood rushing out of his nose.

One day he went next door to this old lady and was acting all nice when suddenly she was gone.

Rebecca Sheppard (12)

Sheldon School, Chippenham

The Predator And The Gazelle

The gazelle pelted across the wild outback with the most deadly predator in the wild. The gazelle skidded to a halt at the edge of a canyon, it drifted to the left as the predator leapt over the edge to plunge to its death.

Bertie Fovargue (11)

Sheldon School, Chippenham

My Cavendish!

Horses come in so many kinds, but one like mine
is hard to find, compared to any other horse. He
is so much quicker and he gives an extremely
loud and encouraging nicker. He gallops so fast,
it really is frightening and goes by the name of Sir
Cavendish Lightning!

Lara Sheate (12)

Sheldon School, Chippenham

The Pebble Pixie

Pixie Path. Dylan looked at the dreary house where he would be staying for the summer. Dylan wandered down the path to the water below. Darkness. A glimmer in the corner of his eye sparkled. Under a pebble the creature winked, buzzed off, and Dylan realised, it was a pixie.

Erin Cottell (12)
The Ladies' College, Guernsey

The Monster

The monster was big, green and slimy. He had yellow teeth, no hair and he stared with not a twinkle in his petrifying eyes, over me. I felt sweat trickle off my forehead and then I looked closer into the monster's eyes, realising the monster was just my older brother!

Stephanie Crame (12)

The Ladies' College, Guernsey

Ride The Beast

It arrived screeching on its brakes. Strapped
in. Front row, white knuckles, excited, heart
thumping against ribcage. It rambled and
rattled, climbing before a death-defying drop.
Whooshing, feeling the wind, hearing people
yelling, screaming, laughing. Inverted 360° loop.
Wheeeee! Corkscrew - mind disorientated,
exhilarating. Let's go again. Ride 'The Beast'.

Gabriella Corlett (12)

The Ladies' College, Guernsey

The Aliens Have Come!

Last night, in the graveyard, I saw a bright light,
like an alien spaceship. The flash lasted a second,
but I knew it was something unusual. I walked
nervously to where the light had come from, and
there stood a hooded figure dressed in black …
The vicar with his torch!

Zosia Damsell (11)

The Ladies' College, Guernsey

The Deep Sea

The diver could see the surface from where he silently swam deep in the murky water. He saw it move and speared it quickly. With that, the blood-stained water bubbled. The diver then swiftly departed, satisfied with his catch.

Meghan De Le Rue (12)

The Ladies' College, Guernsey

The Playground

Boredom struck, so I ran to the playground. I
sat on the swing and flew so high. I got stuck
on the slide and got dizzy on the roundabout. I
went home dirty, with mud in my hair, I needed a
shower to get clean before my mum saw me.

Victoria Duquemin (12)
The Ladies' College, Guernsey

My Mum Woke Me, Thanks A Lot!

The candy was so sweet … I imagined that the sea was fluffy pink marshmallows. Trees had bright yellow trunks and were edible. The leaves were sugary. Even people were edible! My mother and father had green skin. Suddenly my dream ended. My mum woke me, thanks a lot!

Rhiannon Fitch (11)

The Ladies' College, Guernsey

Sweet Heaven

The toffee apple trees dangled with sugar doughnuts and as the chocolate leaves swayed in the strawberry air, the fudge cakes bobbed up and down in the liquorice river. As the wind blew, the lemon drops bounced off the trees and the sugar mice scurried along the rainbow drop path.

Annalise Falla (12)

The Ladies' College, Guernsey

The Lioness' Reward

She was off, darting towards the horrified zebra.
They both ran like rockets over the dry, dusty soil
of the bush. The energetic lioness was catching
up with the ever tiring zebra. She was ready to
pounce. The lioness snatched the zebra off its
feet and started enjoying her reward.

Alice Brown (11)

The Ladies' College, Guernsey

April Fools' Day

Billy went to school. Everything was weird. The school bully, Charles didn't pick on him and the teachers hated him. He even got sent to the principal's office for doing nothing! Billy heard some of his friends laughing at him. Then they shouted, 'April Fools!' It was April Fools' Day!

Annabelle Barnes (11)

The Ladies' College, Guernsey

The Mystical Bus Of Mythical Creatures

The handsome griffin was on the bumpy bus to
Pompeii. An ugly Minotaur boarded with an evil
Centaur. They both elbowed their way up the
aisle. A duel to decide who would get the back
seat commenced. Ducking headbutts and avoiding
kicks the griffin threw them off the bus!

Elizabeth Beacom (12)
The Ladies' College, Guernsey

The Predator

There it was, the predator, a colossal beast. With teeth like nails and fur, white as the snow beneath its feet. It spotted me with eyes as cold as stone. Then I heard a tremendous thud. I closed my eyes hoping to be spared, but the predator got its prey.

Jessica Bell (12)

The Ladies' College, Guernsey

A Demon Child

A demon child. That's what people call Jamie -
why? Wherever he goes, something bad happens.
Last week, Jamie went to the movies. Whilst
watching the film, Jamie got angry. Drinks boiled,
lights exploded and the cinema screen shattered.
Why does this happen to Jamie? No one knows
… except his creator.

Amy Bould (12)
The Ladies' College, Guernsey

307

The Sapphire In Glen

Lina lived right by a huge wood. Once, she ventured in. It was dark beneath the trees. She reached a glen. In the centre lay a sapphire. She was going to pick it up when she saw a woman in the shadows. 'Keep it safe,' she said, and Lina did.

Natasha Brun (12)

The Ladies' College, Guernsey

That One Single Sentence

I watched my world smash and splinter before me. The pieces of fragile memories, that had been forgotten, torn apart, like paper. Hell's furnace gashed and cut me. The magical feeling was ripped away from my heart and pounded into dust. With just that one single sentence, 'I'm dumping you.'

Brittany Chippendale (11)

The Ladies' College, Guernsey

309

The Terror

He swam, circling his prey. He sensed the fear swell up inside of it, deliberately taking as long as possible, to feel the anxiety build up in the prey's mind. Closer, and the terror in its eyes drove him forward. *Snap!* The fish food was no more. Until tomorrow.

Monica Ozanne (11)
The Ladies' College, Guernsey

The Race

The race was intense. All around me people were jostling for first position. I had to avoid sheer drops and slippery banana skins, giant shells and cacti. The race began. *Argh! Whoah! That was close! Bash! Bang! Argh! Oh no!* I'm going to have to start Mario all over again!

Estelle Moseley (11)
The Ladies' College, Guernsey

Garden Of Love

The glistening moon was shining on the rose garden. The stars were like diamonds blazing in the sky. She walked over to him, brushing the petals from the daisies away. He held out his hands as he stepped onto the stand. He knelt down on one knee. He proposed marriage.

Olivia May Younger (12)
The Ladies' College, Guernsey

The Haunted House

'I'm scared,' cried Lisa.
'Don't be such a cry-baby, now hush,' whispered
Laura.
It was a mild winter's night, the town of
Mellowmarsh was covered with a blanket of
crispy white snow. The two girls were exploring
the haunted house. *Whoosh!*
'A ghost!' screamed Lisa.
'Goodbye girls, ha-ha!'

Lauren Sek (12)
The Ladies' College, Guernsey

The Terror From Underneath

Playing in the lake, having fun, not a care in the world. Bare flesh exposed in the water. A sudden scream and a girl disappears. That one bite will have brought the pack. The lake erupts into chaos and people start screaming as they disappear under the water ...

Katie Rowe (12)

The Ladies' College, Guernsey

The Battle

The fairy hollow had long battled the ogre, Bruce.
Today the final fight was due to begin. The chief,
Esmé, rallied her troops. They were armed with
the sharpest weapons they could find. Esmé could
feel her heart beating. The ogre approached.
'Ready, steady, fire!' The battle had begun.

Georgie St Pier (11)
The Ladies' College, Guernsey

315

The Ocean Race

The fish were darting through the ocean, curving and swerving. The great whale was gaining speed. The fish were tiring all too soon. The whale was nearly reaching their tails. A sudden burst of energy and the whale was in front of them. The whale had won the race.

Katie Tradelius (11)

The Ladies' College, Guernsey

Daydream

Looking out the window, counting the cars going by. The cars became sheep flying through the sky. I was with them, touching clouds and feeling the wind on my face. The bell round the sheep's neck didn't stop ringing until I realised it was the school bell. Time for home.

Emilie Payne (11)
The Ladies' College, Guernsey

The Piercing

She's walking towards me with the gun in her hand. She says it'll be painless. I can't look, I'll close my eyes. *Bang! Bang! Bang!* 'Which ones would you like?'

'Silver please.'

It wasn't that bad, it's actually pretty. It didn't hurt having my ears pierced after all.

Olivia Williams (12)

The Ladies' College, Guernsey

The Cactus Attack

I have to save Peach but I'm miles away from her. What can I do? I have found a poisonous blue flower to defend myself. I've got to dodge these giant cacti. I'm nearly there, I can see the castle. *Jump! What? Dead? Nooo!* Now I'll have to start again.

Rebecca Stewart (12)

The Ladies' College, Guernsey

Fairy Land

The cave doors open and I see the most beautiful
place I have witnessed. Fairies everywhere,
flying around then suddenly dancing as if they
rehearsed a production for visitors. Their wings
all fluffy, puffy and sparkling, dancing on rubber
mushrooms, bouncing from one to another, being
as light as feathers.

Lauren Savident (11)
The Ladies' College, Guernsey

The Little Fox

In the dark forest lived a little fox with a little black button nose and one day the little fox went on a big walk. 'Nooo!' said the fox, 'I'm lost!' The little fox wandered for hours and hours until he woke up and found it was all a dream.

Lauren Travers (12)

The Ladies' College, Guernsey

Untitled

A girl got a pumpkin, she brought it home. She went to cut it - she was in dinosaur times! She screamed but the T-rex saw her and ran after her. She looked around and saw the pumpkin on a tree and climbed it! She smashed it and she was home.

Jason Sinfield (12)
William Ellis School, London

Path Of The Jagvos

'So it is true,' Jimmy whispered to the rest of his
squad, 'the path of the Jagvos is here.'
As they crept through the misty wilderness,
sniper fire started coming from everywhere.
They shot back, then bullets ripped through the
snipers' bodies. Then war broke out. Jimmy ran,
shot, killed.

Charlie Sullivan-Jones (12)
William Ellis School, London

Caterpillar Killing Society

Oscar held the caterpillar. It looked up to him and curled into a ball in fright. 'It's all right, I won't hurt you,' said Oscar softly. The caterpillar didn't trust him so it tried to escape and Oscar was just about to let him go when he heard the CKS …

Milo Seery (11)
William Ellis School, London

They

It all started when someone left the window open. They came in and took the boy first, wrapped him up and stole his breath. Then they moved further, Mother, Father, little girl, even the dog. By the morning the family were all wrapped up and dead. Then they moved on.

Emil Torday (11)

William Ellis School, London

325

The Stages Of Life

He was born on a rainy spring day. He found his true love on a sunny afternoon. He became ill on a drafty autumn evening. One shivery winter night he saw his aged mother who gave him the joy of life. He thanked her, and then drifted away, very slowly.

James Lee (11)
William Ellis School, London

Mini Marvels Terrific Tales

Information

We hope you have enjoyed reading this book - and that you will continue to enjoy it in the coming years.

If you like reading and writing, drop us a line or give us a call and we'll send you a free information pack. Alternatively visit our website at **www.youngwriters.co.uk**

Write to:

Young Writers Information,
Remus House,
Coltsfoot Drive,
Peterborough,
PE2 9JX

Tel: (01733) 890066
Email: youngwriters@forwardpress.co.uk